ADDITIONAL PRAISE FOR *WRESTLING STURBRIDGE*

"Beautifully written . . . a chance to be inside the head of a boy just as he becomes a man." **—Pam Conrad, author of *Prairie Songs***

"There are only a few contemporary writers who can hit the mark with teenage boys, and Rich Wallace seems likely to join that group."
—*Chicago Tribune*

"Boys will read this first, and talk about it with their friends. Then they'll talk about it with their fathers, and in times of vulnerability with their girlfriends. Then their friends, their fathers and their girlfriends will read it. This book will be around for a long time."
—Chris Crutcher, author of *Ironman*

"Excellent. . . . The story is well told and very well written."
—*The New Yorker*

"Here's a contender—tough, smart, all the right moves. With his first novel, Rich Wallace vaults into the first string with Bruce Brooks and Chris Crutcher. This is a complex, hard-edged story that boys will want to—love to—read." **—Robert Lipsyte, author of *The Contender*
and columnist for *The New York Times***

"The author tells a terrific story—subtle, funny, cleanly drawn."
—*Los Angeles Times Book Review*

"Wallace limns the pleasures and limitations of small-town culture with a sure hand . . . a strong debut." **—*Kirkus Reviews***

"The story is really exciting, and Ben is just the kind of sweet-but-determined guy you wish you knew." **—*Seventeen***

ALSO AVAILABLE IN LAUREL-LEAF BOOKS:

ATHLETIC SHORTS, *Chris Crutcher*
RUNNING LOOSE, *Chris Crutcher*
BRIAN'S RETURN, *Gary Paulsen*
BROKEN CHORDS, *Barbara Snow Gilbert*
THE LIKES OF ME, *Randall Beth Platt*
THE HERMIT THRUSH SINGS, *Susan Butler*
BURNING UP, *Caroline B. Cooney*
MIND'S EYE, *Paul Fleischman*
THE SPRING TONE, *Kazumi Yumoto*
NOBODY ELSE HAS TO KNOW, *Ingrid Tomey*

RICH WALLACE

WRESTLING STURBRIDGE

LAUREL-LEAF
BOOKS

Published by
Dell Laurel-Leaf
an imprint of
Random House Children's Books
a division of Random House, Inc.
1540 Broadway
New York, New York 10036

Visit us on the Web! www.randomhouse.com/teens

**Educators and librarians, for a variety of teaching tools, visit us at
www.randomhouse.com/teachers**

ISBN: 0-679-88555-2

RL: 6.5

Reprinted by arrangement with Alfred A. Knopf,
a division of Random House, Inc.

Printed in the United States of America

First Laurel-Leaf edition May 2001

10 9 8 7 6

OPM

*FOR MY FATHER
AND MY SONS*

WRESTLING
STURBRIDGE

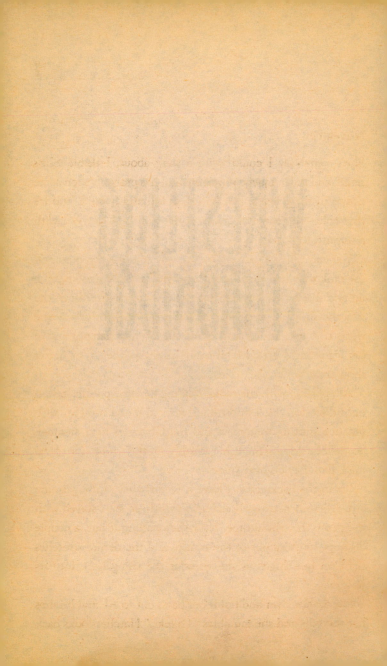

CHAPTER 1

November

She's somebody I could write a song about, I think. She's small, and older, maybe nineteen, and has probably seen some things in those years. Her hair is so full and bouncy, and it's that color—a couple of colors, really—of dried hay, but with a warmth to it, too.

You can tell she's strong by the way she lifts the pump off the tank with one lean, flexed arm and flips that handle thing up and shakes her hair off her face. There's authority in the way she shoves it smoothly into the car and in the way she wears that mechanic's shirt, gray with the tail hanging out of her jeans and a little Mobil patch on the pocket. It's a better show than MTV.

Al's playing with the radio, looking for the Spanish station out of Weston. He's in an international mood tonight, with practice starting tomorrow and the Olympics next summer. So we'll be driving English, probably, on the wrong side of the road, like they do over there.

I'm in the backseat so I have a decent view of the gasoline girl. Al's only getting three bucks' worth, so she's stayed with the pump the whole time. Now she's pulling it out, a couple of drops spurting out of the nozzle, and the denim stretches tight on her thighs as she wrestles the thing back into its holster.

She ambles over and holds her hand out to Al, and he slips her the bills and she mumbles "Thanks." Hatcher looks back at Digit and smirks, and I don't know if they know something about this girl or what.

Al pulls out kind of fast and I look back and she's already got the pump in another car, a van, actually, and she's reaching over to get one of those squeegee things out of a bucket.

We didn't bother going to the football game. It's the last game, but we're all in our own worlds tonight and didn't want any distractions. And I've avoided public places since I beat up that minister.

We hit the mats for real tomorrow morning, so Digit's mostly looking out the window at the town's dark stores and Hatcher's steadily squeezing a rubber ball to build up his forearms, as if they're not built up enough already.

Al's the only one who's really saying anything, and he's just been going on about kicking people's butts and winning the state meet. He found the station, so now he's beating on the dashboard and singing words he doesn't understand. My right shoulder still hurts a little.

The town is deserted—even more deserted than most nights—because everybody who'd be hanging out is at the game. In an hour the usual spots will be filled—strategic storefronts and benches.

In this car with me are my three best friends, and the three biggest obstacles to my doing much wrestling this winter. I have weighed 135 pounds for two solid years now. After Thanksgiving dinner and a pint of ice cream I might balloon up to 135½ for a few minutes, and if I run eight miles hard in the middle of the summer I might shed a pound or two of water.

I am a natural 135-pounder. So is Al. The other two—Digit and Hatcher, I mean—could be among the best in the state this season at 130 and 140.

We call him Digit because he's missing one—he's got no pinkie on his right hand. But I don't think it's ever made any difference to him. We always said if he couldn't make weight for a match then he could just cut off the other one.

We're outside of town now, heading for Weston, I guess. There's no traffic, so Al takes it over to the other lane and puts on a proper British accent.

"Bloody good driving, if I do say so," he says, holding his arms straight out on the wheel like a chauffeur or something. He swings back over into the American lane and turns up the radio.

It doesn't take long to get away from town, and then it's twenty minutes, mostly through the woods, until you get into Weston. Our town is small—about four thousand people, plus all the farms on the outskirts—but it's the county seat, so we've got the courthouse and the jail and an abnormally high concentration of lawyers. Most of the guys who work, work at Sturbridge Building Products, making cinder blocks, precast concrete steps, stuff like that. That's where my father works. And Al's father and Digit's. Hatcher's old man is a doctor, but he's president of the Wrestling Boosters Association. They've got about four hundred members. I'm not kidding.

Part of me wishes we'd gone to the game so I could look for this junior that I sit near in geometry. She's cute and doesn't have a boyfriend or anything, and I'm pretty sure she doesn't mind that I'm a wrestler. I mentioned her to Hatcher the other day, and he sort of frowned and said, "What are you interested in a spic for?" I had no answer at the time.

There's about three levels of girls at the school—some who are almost groupies about the wrestlers (not very many of them, and they're mostly annoying); some who are anti-wrestling because, I have to admit, the whole town is a little warped about the sport; and the ones in the middle who judge us for what we're worth.

If you wonder why I'm taking geometry as a senior, it's because it took me three years to get through two years of algebra. And, to use an algebra expression (I don't use very many), the missing factor in the girl thing I stated above is that there are a whole lot of girls who probably don't even give half a thought about whether somebody wrestles or not. I have to keep that in mind.

There seems to be an important announcement on the radio. I catch the word for "dictator," I think, and then the guy clearly says "Honduras." Hatcher yawns and stretches in the front seat and says he's getting tired. Al punches one of the things you punch to change the station in a hurry, and we get Top 40 music out of Scranton.

"Doughnuts," says Al, looking around and nodding. Digit says the same thing, and I nod, too. Mr. Donut is about our best road trip. There's a doughnut place in town, but we like the ride to Weston and Mr. Donut gives us a valid reason to go. I've puked doughnuts out the window twice on the way back. Doughnuts and Rolling Rock. (My limit ought to be three beers, but I can't stop at an odd number.)

Us four have our differences, but mostly we see eye to eye. We all want the same thing.

Two guys from Sturbridge have won state titles over the years. Jerry Franken won at 135—my weight—about twenty years and seventy pounds ago, and now he's a supervisor at the plant and treasurer of the booster club.

Peter Valdez managed to dry out to 103 as a senior six years ago and went undefeated. We were in sixth grade that year and were just getting into wrestling. That's when the four of us hooked up, became a unit. We'd go wild at the matches— Peter pinned just about everybody he faced. We wanted to be just like him.

Peter got a full ride to Pitt and made All-America as a freshman, then screwed up his knee and quit school.

My dad says Peter should get promoted to supervisor any day now.

Al almost hit a deer right around here last time we went to Weston. It raced out into the road and then froze in the headlights. If we'd been on the right side of the road, we would've nailed it, but it got out of the way just in time. It was a buck; looked like a four-point but we didn't get a good look. Scared the piss out of us. This area is overrun with deer.

Except when I go hunting. Then the deer disappear.

My dad gets a deer just about every season. I've been hunting with a bow for four years and haven't even taken a shot. "You're not patient enough, Benny," he says.

We come over the hill and can see Weston lit up in the valley. It's big enough to be considered "the city" around here—there's a real downtown with exotic things like movie theaters and three-story buildings. In Sturbridge we've got a McDonald's and an Arthur Treacher's, a strip mall with an Acme, an anemic Kmart, about seven shoe stores, and several video places. People drive over to Weston to keep from going insane with boredom.

Weston has two high schools: North and South. They're both in our conference, and they beat up on us pretty good in most sports. Not wrestling. Wearing a Sturbridge wrestling jacket carries some weight over here, although we don't go looking for fights. Hatcher's the only one of us who usually wears his letterman's jacket anyway.

Al parks at Mr. Donut, which is pretty much empty. There's two girls at the counter who might be from the college (it's called Weston Area Community College), but they don't look very receptive. And like I said, we're not looking for distractions. We get our stuff quietly and head across the parking lot to the Burger King.

One of Al's best tricks is to get a milkshake and fill his mouth with it, then go out in the parking lot and make believe he's puking it up. You can ruin a lot of people's meals that way. Tonight we're quiet though, pensive I think the word is. Tomorrow we hit the mats.

Al is picking at his hair with one of those big-toothed combs as we start back. He got it cut this afternoon, or shorn, because his hair is kind of like a sheep's, really curly. He looks evil, with the same kind of tight hair on his chin and above his lip (that's the only place he can grow it) and a mocking kind of smile. But he's okay. His father is one of the few people ever to get fired from the plant, because he drinks more than anybody else and controls it even less. They rehired him last winter. Al was 11–0 at the time.

I don't know what else to say. Practice starts in about ten hours. I'll be spending the year getting pushed into the mat by Al in workouts and watching the meets from the sidelines. If I cut weight or add it, I run into Hatcher and Digit.

I just look out the window all the way back to Sturbridge and hardly say a word.

The needle's on empty when we get back to town, but Al drives right past the Mobil station, which stays open until midnight. The girl is standing on the island with her back to the road, looking at her nails, I think. I figure she weighs about a hundred and six.

She's somebody I could probably write a song about.

The worst things about Sturbridge:

  * there's nothing to do

  * there's no way out

  * there's no end in sight

The best:

  * the wrestling team

  * the cinder blocks

  * you can smell cows from my bedroom
    when the ground thaws in spring

My father sits awake most nights until one or two, not really waiting up for me. Just waiting, I guess.

"Go to the game?" he asks as I walk into the living room. He leans forward in his armchair, the tan one that almost matches the sofa they bought when they got married. He's drinking a pint can of Schaefer, but he's not drunk.

"Nah," I say. "We just hung out. Too keyed up."

"Well, tomorrow's the day," he says, knowing what I mean. He looks back at the TV—*Cheers* in syndication. "This is your year, Benny."

It isn't, but I nod and kind of suck in my lips. What he doesn't know is that Hatcher isn't at 145 anymore, and Al didn't bulk up to 140, like we planned. So instead of a block of the four of us from 130 to 145, it's only three, with me as the odd man out.

"Mom asleep?" I ask.

"Yeah."

My father works hard—you can see it in his face. He's lean, like me, but his eyes are tired and he ought to wash his hair more often. He just seems to have shrunk into his body sort of, like there was an extra layer of muscle under the skin that melted away and now the skin's a little too loose. He never wrestled. Played baseball at Sturbridge twenty-five years ago, and still plays softball in a summer league and goes bowling once a week. Does a job once in a while at night, on the sly.

He leans back in his chair and looks at me with something

like pride, expecting, I guess, that he'll soon have a reason to be proud of me. He doesn't pressure me, ever. But I've seen the way he looks when I win, trying to contain his smile and not yelling much, even if it isn't a varsity match. I know it'd make him the proudest guy in town if I was winning regularly.

Like lots of others in this town, my father envisions us as this solid, unbeatable block; four straight weight classes worth four pins in nearly every match. The kind of nucleus that wins championships. The fact that we've been friends for so long makes it that much sweeter. At least in theory.

Suddenly, there's not as much room in that theory. Suddenly, I'm not really sure who I've been friends with. Can you be best friends with a group?

You have to realize that I've been wrestling against Al since junior high school, and I haven't beaten him in three years. If he wasn't such a borderline student, he could go anywhere he wants next year.

Then there's Hatcher up at 140. A year ago I could probably take him, even giving away a lot of weight, but a year ago he was just a little better than average (third in the district) at 145. He's dropped weight since then, went to two camps last summer (Trenton and Penn State), wrestled in all-comers tournaments, and improved two hundred percent. And if I could dry out to 130 (I just get weak as hell), Digit would kick my butt, too.

I sigh out of frustration, but turn it into a yawn. I'm not giving up on myself, and I'll never quit trying. But if you look at this with any objectivity at all, then you know I've got just about nowhere to go this season. "See you tomorrow, Dad," I say, and head up the stairs.

My father yawns and pulls one foot up on the chair with him, and blinks a couple of times. "Go get 'em," he says.

Those are the same words I heard him whisper last month when I went after the minister.

Some things I won't eat:

* sushi

* lamb

* cheese

* baloney

Some things that I will:

* rice

* oranges

* chicken

* pretzels

I've got ten minutes. We've been at it for more than an hour, and there's at least that much to go, and you can bet this is the only break he's gonna give us.

So far it's been okay. We've been going one-on-one for about twenty minutes, and of course I'm matched with Al. He's only pinned me twice, but he's been in control most of the way.

My shoulder's all right; it only hurts when Al's got leverage and I'm trying to stay off my back. He knows it hurts, and he's got every right to exploit that. He hasn't pinned me because of the pain, just because he's stronger.

There's a frantic kind of energy because we know how good we can be this year. We're solid at every weight class except heavyweight, and there's competition two or three deep for every spot except Al's and Digit's and Hatcher's. Maybe Al will have some competition.

Hatcher is over by the window, getting some air, and he sees me leaning here by the water fountain. "Getting your ass kicked?" he wants to know, and I shrug and say, "Yeah, but not entirely." He comes over and I get another drink.

He asks me how I'm doing, how many times I got pinned, and if I managed to score any points. I tell him, but I'm staring at the wall and getting my head together while I'm talking, thinking about maybe cutting weight.

There are about eight freshmen sprawled on the floor about ten feet away from us in the hall. Coach goes extra tough on freshmen, especially in the first couple of weeks, so you can't stay with this program unless you really, really want to.

"Get up, girls," Hatcher says to them, and they all get up in a pretty big hurry because you don't screw around with a wrestling star in this town. You just don't.

Hatcher gets one of them in a headlock, a little kid with big ears and kind of a bowl haircut. "What's your name?" he asks.

"Tom Austin," the kid says, smiling like he's thinking maybe Hatcher's just being friendly.

"No. It's not. Not this season," Hatcher says. "It's Susan." He lets the kid go. There's a fat kid standing there looking dumb and scared in a purple T-shirt, and Hatcher grabs one of his nipples and starts twisting. The kid jerks back, but Hatcher holds tight and laughs. When he lets go, the kid looks around at the other freshmen, mostly just embarrassed. "You'll be Claudia," Hatcher says.

Hatcher heads back for the gym and I start to follow. I turn to Tommy Austin, who I know from church and because our mothers are friends. He gives me a raised-eyebrows look because he's a tough enough kid and senses that this is part of the game.

"Hatcher was Eleanor for the first month of the season when we were freshmen," I tell him. The fat kid is holding his nipple, and I'm pretty sure he's not going to make it. "I was Princess."

The kid smiles a little.

We get back to the gym and the coach splits me and Al up so we can work with younger guys. We're working on takedowns, and I've got fat Claudia in my group. He's soft, like he's never wrestled before, so it's like wrestling one of those blow-up punching bags with a Bozo face or something. Then we do leg lifts and very slow push-ups and other painful exercises for about a half hour, and hit the showers. A lot of guys look just about dead.

I reach into my locker and wipe my face on a T-shirt, sitting there in a jockstrap and still breathing extra. Al is six feet away, telling some of the new guys that you have to hate your opponent, you have to crush him or he'll do the same to you. You never let up, he says, and he's right, but he's looking hard at me and I don't feel like looking back. I take a bottle of shampoo from the shelf in my locker and strip off the jock, then pick up my towel and head for the shower.

There's a wall of steam coming from the shower area, and about twenty-seven guys are crammed in there under the ten showerheads. Hatcher's facing the shower in the corner, so his butt is toward me. Hatcher's almost square, he's so muscular, and the almost crewcut exaggerates his Marine look. Al isn't so much muscular as angular, with just the right balance and flexibility.

Hatcher's got his eyes closed, so I reach over and turn off the hot water and turn up the cold. He jumps and laughs and tells me I suck, then he grabs a freshman and holds him under the cold water. I duck under another shower and get my hair wet. Hatcher gets bored with the freshman, takes a piss on the wall, and walks out into the locker room.

I get back to my locker and Coach is sitting there on the bench, talking to Al. He turns to me and points, but keeps talking to Al. "This is the reason nobody'll beat you this year," he says. "Benny is the best workout partner you could get."

I give him a tight smile, and he swings his legs over the bench so they're on my side. He's about thirty-five and paunchy. He wrestled down at East Stroudsburg State and works out with the upper-weight guys now. He leans in like he's about to confide something to me, taking his lower lip between his teeth and squinting some.

"You'll get your matches," he says. "Al and Hatch will need some work against heavier guys, so they'll shift up a weight sometimes and you'll handle 135."

"Let him wrestle JV," says Al, who's been listening the whole time, drying his frizzy hair with a towel. "Seniors on other teams do it all the time."

"No way," he says. "No seniors go JV in this school. You know that."

"I wouldn't want to," I say. I was 16–0 JV last winter and won a holiday tournament, but I'm not looking for consolation this year. I look at Al, then at the coach, then I turn my head to my locker. They're both full of shit if they think I'm going to accept being a backup. I want to be state champion just as much as Al does.

There's a party tonight, mostly because of the end of football season, but any excuse for a party will do around here. I think I'm up for it. We all get dried and dressed and pile into Al's car—me and Hatcher and Digit and Al. I keep telling myself that I've won forty-two high school matches and lost only five (even though it's mostly been JV), and you never know who might get hurt. The coach has me listed second on the depth chart at 135 and 140, and if I really dry out, I might still have a shot at Digit down at 130. Something has to give. I'm not going to watch these guys have all the fun.

Places I want to go:

* Iceland, because it's isolated

* New Orleans during Mardi Gras

* Penn State on a wrestling
  scholarship

* Kim's house

Places I don't:

* Staten Island, because it's
  in New York

* Australia, because it's so
  far from everything

* prison

* the Middle East

Al is one of the school's biggest drinkers, but he's sitting at the kitchen table tonight with a two-liter bottle of Pepsi in front of him. The other guys at the table are mostly football players, and they're sucking down beers like we would do if it wasn't wrestling season.

Parties like this one are tense if you're not drinking. I can't talk to girls much unless I get my tongue loosened first. Kim is here, the one from geometry, but she's in a corner with some other girls, laughing and drinking wine coolers.

We got here twenty minutes ago, and Al has said something about his not drinking at least four times. Then he confides in whoever's closest that there's a pint of vodka mixed in with the Pepsi, and we're all just so stunned we can hardly stand it.

Digit's got a new pair of pants on and he's wearing shoes, which is unusual for him (leather shoes, I mean, like for church or something—he almost always wears sneakers). He's decided to be mature all of a sudden; got his hair cut short and acts polite. He's sitting next to me on a kitchen counter, chewing gum.

There's not a whole lot of room in this house (this is where one of the cheerleaders lives; her parents are out of town at a funeral), and anybody who's cool, borderline cool, or knows somebody that's cool is here. That's just about every senior and junior and some sophomores. A couple of extremely hot-looking freshman girls are along. That's about the whole guestlist.

If the party follows the usual script, then a handful of last year's seniors will show up later on, very drunk and still wearing their lettermen's jackets, and there'll be one or two arguments and a couple of punches. I could be involved, but usually I'm not.

Kim comes into the kitchen, squeezing through the crowd, and I look sideways at Digit. He's sitting with his hands on his knees, looking around. Since he got his hair cut, it's lighter, almost red, and his ears stick out. He doesn't say much, but he's deep. Every once in a while he shows evidence of that. Not lately, though.

Kim has on a dark sweater and black jeans. She's got a healthy tone to her skin, which looks good with dark hair. Five three; weighs about a hundred; no excess. She's looking for another wine cooler, which could be in my favor. She hasn't seen me yet. She's got a thin silver chain around her neck, which I like, and she shows an athleticism that could be useful. She runs cross-country and track, which is good for the legs.

Digit nudges me and stares at Al over at the table. I can only catch part of what Al is saying because the music's sort of loud, but he's talking to Richie Foster, who's a junior and looks like he'll be our man at 189, and pointing to the Pepsi bottle. Richie heads into the living room and Al turns to right tackle Ernie Corso and tells him again that the Pepsi isn't just Pepsi. Everybody laughs real hard.

"Hi, Ben." Kim's standing in front of me, very friendly looking. "Hi, Digit," she says, too.

She hands me a bottle and asks me to open it, and that

seems like an excuse to come over, but I'm not complaining. It doesn't open as easy as it ought to, but I get the cap off.

"How's it going?" she says.

"Great," I answer. I nod my head to reinforce what I said.

"You like this song?" she says, pointing to the CD player.

I hadn't really thought about it. But I figure she must like it, since she asked. "Yeah," I say. "I like it."

"I listen to these guys a lot," she says. "They get me psyched before I run." She looks out into the living room, where a few people are dancing. She looks back at me and just rotates her shoulders slightly. "I have most of their tapes."

I can think of absolutely nothing to say, so I just nod with my mouth hanging open. She looks back into the living room, then takes the bottle from me. "Well . . . thanks," she says with a smile. She punches Digit playfully in the knee, then heads back for the corner where her friends are.

I look at my hand, which has a little ring of cuts on it in the shape of the wine cooler cap.

Digit smirks and grins at me. "Smooth" is all he says. Like I said, he's deep. He can say an awful lot in a word or two, like "Nice going, jerk, she's standing there looking great and giving you an obvious opening with that lame 'Open this bottle, please, you big strong man' thing, and you just nod your head like a goof and let her get away." He said all that and more with just a look and a single word from the fifties: smooth. I often wish I could be that eloquent.

We drink sometimes, me and Digit, but not to lose ourselves. It's great in the early fall on a really crisp evening to get a bottle or some beers and sit in the woods, up past my house or in the cemetery. When the four of us get drunk together, we might act like jerks, but if Hatcher isn't around—when it's just me and Al and Digit—we can get down to some serious stuff.

One night, maybe two weeks ago, we sat under the stars till really late, talking about getting out of here next summer, maybe going out West. Al said he'd like to work in the rodeo. He's never been on a horse, I don't think. But you say things like that when you're really relaxed, when you know you can get away with it. If Hatcher had heard that, he'd never let Al forget it; he'd be calling him Tex or something. But I get it, and so does Digit, even if it's not really about the rodeo or working on a fishing boat or going to Wyoming. It's about getting out. Breaking the pattern.

You can't talk about things like that at a kitchen table with everybody in school here, trying to be cool.

I hop off the counter and squeeze through the crowd to the refrigerator. I get a can of 7-Up for me and one for Digit (he doesn't really want one, but I have this thing about balance, and if he drinks one too it will be even). I come back over to the counter and sit down again. That took about two minutes, maybe less.

"Seen Hatcher?" I ask.

Digit says he thinks Hatcher's upstairs already with Marcie, a cheerleader who just broke up with Andy Larson, the quarterback. Hatcher and Andy are pretty good friends, though, so that shouldn't cause much trouble. Plus Hatcher could kick the shit out of Andy if it came to that.

I can see through the doorway into the living room, where

Kim is. And I notice that Marcie is there, too. "Marcie's out in the living room," I say to Digit. He says, "Oh." Andy's at the table with Al. Al's already getting kind of loud. Me or Digit'll have to drive his car home, which is something we do a lot.

About an hour later I finally get around to talking to Kim out on the back porch. I saw her slip out there, probably for some air because a lot of people are smoking in here, so I get down from the counter and tell Digit I'll be right back.

"How's it going?" I ask. I think I asked her that before, but it's been an hour and things might have changed.

"Great," she says, which is pretty much how it was last time. "Want a sip of this?" she asks, holding up a bottle.

"Nah," I say. "We don't drink in season."

"Oh," she says and smiles. She chugs down the rest of the bottle (maybe two ounces) and shows me the label. It's non-alcoholic cranberry sparkler. There's a tiny pink drop of it on her lip. She sets the bottle on the railing and flicks back her hair, which is medium long and sometimes gets in her eyes. There's no light on the porch, but there's quite a bit of light from the kitchen, so we're not standing in the dark. It's stopped raining.

"How's wrestling going?" she asks.

"Well, this was the first day," I say. For once I don't want to talk about wrestling. "So it's hard to say. Things look good. How's things with you? You been running?"

"Five a day," she says. "I'm going easy right now, getting my head back together. I'll step up my mileage soon."

I don't know a whole lot about cross-country. I know she won the league meet but bombed in the states.

"You ready for that test?" she asks.

"Not yet." I definitely don't want to talk about geometry. What do I want to talk about? Al saves me from worrying about that for long.

He comes out and puts his arms around Kim from behind. He barely knows her, but I guess he figures that anything of mine is also his by association. She turns and gives him a kind of puzzled look, but she's not annoyed or anything. "Hi, Al," she says.

He keeps an arm around her shoulder and says to her that I'm the key man in his life right now. "You gotta push me," he says to me. "If I'm gonna win the states, I gotta work my ass off every day."

Kim slowly twists out of his grasp, and Al puts his hands on my shoulders. He's drunk, and there's this sudden surge coming over him. "Nobody's gonna touch me this season," he says with his teeth clenched, smiling at me. "You gotta make me work, Benny, you gotta make me work."

Then he's got a hand on my thigh and he's taking me down, right there in the muddy backyard. And before I know it I'm on my back, and he's got me cradled and I can't do anything about it.

"Guys, stop," Kim says. "Come on." But Al's got me pinned down and there's mud all over my back. He backs off and I get up on my knees, then he's on me again, shouting "Two, two." (That's how many points you get for a takedown.)

"Al, cut the shit," I say, with my cheek pressed into the dirt and my arm twisted behind my back. "That's my bad shoulder, asshole."

He gets up and pulls me to my feet and I shove him away.

"You gotta work my butt off, Benny," he says. "You gotta get me that championship."

He goes back into the house. There's about six guys on the porch watching. Kim is shaking her head. "What's wrong with him?" she says when I come over.

"He's . . . got problems, I guess." I wipe the back of my head with my hand, then wipe the mud from my hand onto my jacket. "I gotta go home and change."

"Are you going to come back?" I think I hear some hope in her voice.

"I don't know. Maybe not."

But I go home and take a shower and change and do another hundred sit-ups, and since it's still pretty early, my father says I can use the car if I'm not drinking. "Get some gas while you're at it," he says from his chair, handing me a ten. So I pull out of the driveway and debate whether to go back to the party or just drive around by myself. There's about a quarter tank of gas in the wagon, so I can get away with thirty or forty miles, I figure.

It's downhill from my house to the party, which is on the other end of town. You can walk from one side of Sturbridge to the other in ten minutes, and drive it in two. There's two traffic lights, one on either end of Main Street: up where it crosses the Pocono River and down at our end, up Monroe Street from the plant. We live two blocks up the other side of Monroe, which puts us just about out of town.

Sturbridge is very compact—tightly spaced houses with narrow driveways, small yards with thick trees overhead—then the land spreads out quickly when the houses end. There's a dairy farm about two hundred yards up the road from our house, and the road turns to dirt another quarter mile along. When I hunt, I just go out the back door, cross my neighbor's yard, and walk a couple hundred yards to the woods.

I pull up to the party, and Kim and Digit and surprisingly Marcie are sitting on the front steps, waiting for me, I think. They come over and get in, and Marcie's wearing Digit's Red Barons cap. They get in the back and Kim gets in next to me.

"Get the mud out of your hair?" Digit says.

I smirk back at him and show him that my hair's still wet from the shower, and I say "What a jerk," meaning Al, but I say it in a way that doesn't have any bitterness, I think.

"He was wasted," Digit says. "When he came back in, he stood on the kitchen table and told everybody he just won the Olympic gold medal. He started singing 'The Star-Spangled Banner.'"

I put the radio on; we only have AM in this car and the only station that comes in clear is country-western. I'm surprised that Digit's sitting so close to Marcie, who only cheers during football season because she plays forward on the basketball team. She's good-looking and athletic, and she's on that plane a little above me and Digit, in the most popular fringe. Hatcher and Al have started crossing into that fringe at times, but me and Digit have always been a notch below.

Kim's not sitting close to me at all, which is okay since I haven't earned it yet. "I miss anything?" I ask.

"Darla broke up with Eddie," Kim says with not much enthusiasm. "Ernie won a chugging contest." She looks at me and kind of rolls her eyes. "I can only take so much of that nonsense."

We've already covered the whole length of Main Street, and I stop at the light where it dead-ends into Route 6 above the plant. The usual routine here is to make a left and loop back around the block, heading up Main Street in the opposite direction. You follow the same general pattern when you reach the other end of Main, and in this fashion you can be sure to keep up with all the major developments outside the Turkey Hill Market and the Rite Aid drugstore, which are the only places in town open past dinnertime. (The McDonald's, Kmart, and a few other places are out on 6, about a half mile away from the business district. Those establishments are not so essential that they need to be included in every loop; every fifth or sixth time is sufficient.) Rite Aid closes at ten, Turkey Hill at one.

The Sturbridge National Bank keeps its digital clock on all night. Right now it's 10:51 and 42 degrees. Although we rarely talk about it, just about every kid in town has a pretty good awareness of time and temperature because of that clock. You could argue that those awarenesses contribute in some way to our wrestling success. But you'd probably lose the argument.

Kim is twisting her hair around her finger and looking out the window, and I think Digit is actually trying to make out with Marcie.

I don't regularly talk much, but it seems I ought to be forcing along a conversation with Kim. I want to ask her to run six miles a day instead of five, or six one day and four the next. And I want to ask her what's going on with Digit and Marcie, because I sure as hell never saw that coming, but that'll have to wait.

So we don't say a whole lot as I slowly drive four regular loops and two extended ones. I read the signs out on Route 6 for the thousandth time: Just listed—3 bedrooms on lake, $69,900; Sturbridge Greenhouse; Live Bait-Nightcrawlers-Always Fresh; Friday-Satday Special ROAST CHICKEN MASH POTATO 5.99; Dodge Trucks; AGWAY; Mike's Video—BUY AMERICAN, SAVE JOBS.

The radio's going and there are a lot of younger kids downtown—freshmen and sophomores mostly, hanging out in front of stores, wishing they had something to do. The biggest group is in front of the movie theater, which shut down about six years ago and has been vacant ever since. The cops will chase them away any minute now. There's a place called The Fun Zone out at the strip mall next to Kmart, with pinball and video games, but it's not cool to hang out there if you're over twelve. They do have a couple of pool tables, though.

Nobody wants anything at McDonald's. We go past the party house again, and Digit says, "You better let us out. I'll get Al and drive him home."

Digit and Marcie get out and I'm left with Kim. After a minute she asks, "Why is Al so important to you guys?"

"I don't know." I shrug. "We watch out for each other."

I really don't know why. "Maybe it's because he's got potential the rest of us don't quite have, and we can't bear to see it wasted," I say. I start chewing on my lip, not really sure about this. Why should I care about Al? If he wastes his chance, it just opens the door for me.

Kim looks confused, too. "If he can't control himself, why should you guys even try?"

"I don't know. It's sort of . . . nobody else is looking out for him. It's just Al and his father at home, and his father is kind of lost. I think Al spends time looking out for him, instead of the other way around. And he's not so out of control, really. He's as dedicated as the rest of us."

"Didn't look that way tonight," she says, but she seems amused rather than critical.

"We've been wrestling together since sixth grade, so we know where we stand with each other," I say. "We all work hard, we all want to be the best we can, but Al's got talents the rest of us can only think about. Great balance, unbelievable flexibility, and this ability to anticipate what the other guy's going to do."

Kim thinks about this a second, then gives me a half smile. "I've seen you wrestle, Ben," she says. "Don't sell yourself short."

It's 11:38 when we get back to Main Street (I had figured 11:36) and it's dropped a degree to 41. Kim waves to a guy who's standing under the clock with a bunch of his friends, guys who graduated two years ago. "My neighbor," she says to me. "Jess. You know him?"

"A little," I answer. "Not much."

"He's smart," she says. "I don't know why he's still hanging around Sturbridge."

"This is where he lives," I say. "He lives here."

"He's twenty."

"I guess." I'm not sure what she's getting at. He shouldn't live here because he's twenty? I mean, I want to get out too, but it's not so easy. "So where do you expect to be?" I say. "When you're twenty."

"Villanova, I hope. Or Stanford."

"Oh." I think she really means it. It makes sense. More sense than the rodeo. We don't say anything for a few more blocks. Then Kim yawns and says she'd better get home, and I do still have to get gasoline. She lives over past the hospital, I'm not sure exactly where, but I turn toward the river in that direction.

"It's the third one on the right," she says when we get to Ridge Street, and I pull up there and she does a surprising thing. She slides up close to me and kisses me on the cheek, and I can't see how I deserve that. "That's for being such a nice guy," she says. She looks at me like she wants to say something else, then finally she does. "Loosen up, okay?"

She says goodnight and gets out of the car, and I'm not sure if she means I should loosen up with her, or with Al, or what. I'll have to think about it.

I watch her walk away, and I kind of shudder. She seems to

have me pretty well figured out, even if I haven't got a clue myself.

There's a Texaco at the corner by the light, but I think I can get it cheaper out on 6. So I head down Main Street one last time and drive out beyond the plant and the Kmart and McDonald's.

She's there, wearing a heavy gray sweatshirt with the hood pulled up, and there's only one other car at the pumps. But she's at that car, and it'll look pretty odd if I pull up behind her and wait. There's a fuzzy older guy standing on the open side, and I know he'll be filling my car if I pull over there. I consider driving up the road a mile or so and coming back when she's free, but I've already turned into the station so I just say the hell with it and go to the other side.

I roll down the window and tell the guy to give me ten regular, and at least I have a good look at the girl. The other car is already pulling away, and if I'd been thirty seconds later I could be over there now, talking to her. She doesn't look my way, standing there counting bills.

She steps over to the back of my car to talk to the older guy, who runs the place, and I can see her from mid-thigh up to neck level in my side-view mirror. Miraculously, the phone starts ringing inside the station, and the guy rushes over to get it. "He's getting ten," he yells to the girl, which means she'll be completing the transaction. I get a surge of adrenaline, like when they call you onto the mat for a match.

She takes the pump out and hangs it up and screws the gas cap back in place. "Okay," she says with a really sweet smile, and I hand her the ten. I can smell gasoline on her hands. She takes the bills out of her pocket and folds the ten around the wad.

"How's business tonight?" I say, surprising even myself.

She tilts her head and brushes some stray hair back into her hood. "Regular," she says.

"Cold," I say.

"Not too bad," she says. "We're outta here in ten minutes."

"Yeah," I say. I start the engine.

"'Night," she says and turns to a guy in a pickup truck who's pulled up on the other side. I wave to her.

I turn back onto 6 and turn up the volume on the radio, but I keep the window open and lean my elbow out. "Wooooo," I say, pretty loud, feeling really good all of a sudden. Feeling pumped up. Thinking about Al.

Flexibility is one thing, balance is another, and strength and instinct are essential. But desire is something you can't place a value on. Desire can overcome all those other things, can turn a sheep into a tiger. Loosen up, I tell myself. Want it. Want it more than he does.

I'm gonna kick his butt on Monday. And I'm gonna come back and talk to this girl again.

My best matches:

  * won final of East Pocono JV
    Tournament by pin

  * freshman year, pinned guy from
    Wharton in 18 seconds

  * last year, lost wrestle-off to
    Al, 9-4

My worst:

  * got pinned in first period vs.
    Laurelton last year

  * puked on mat after winning a match
    two years ago

  * lost first-ever varsity match, 13-3

Not sure:

  * church league soccer game last
    month--hit that pompous,
    hypocritical jerk with a couple of
    good ones before they dragged us
    apart; thought I'd be going to jail

Sunday afternoons my father's mother comes over for dinner and to watch "Pocono Polka" at six. She doesn't have cable at her house.

By six my father's ready for cheese and beer, and the three of them sit in the living room to watch people from up the valley dance to the best polka bands around. I usually stand at the edge of the room, trying to prod myself to leave but staring at the set, mesmerized as if witnessing a horrible accident: Puffy women in "Lackawanna Polka Dots" jackets dancing with their sisters, and stiff old guys in polyester bowling shirts with big guts. They televise this, I swear.

Probably the last time my parents danced was when my aunt got married ten years ago.

A commercial comes on, and I go out in the kitchen. The oven-stuffer chicken is still sitting on the counter, and I bend down to get a sheet of foil to cover it. My grandmother comes in and yanks a hunk off the bird and shoves it in her mouth. "Best part about a chicken is snitching some later," she says.

Yeah, Grandma. And it's real appetizing for the rest of us when you get your fingers in there, too.

"Good strong sermon this morning," she says to me with a tight smile.

The sermon seemed to be about vulgarity, and obscenity, and adultery, and hanging out on Main Street at night. The key thing you have to know about this town is that it disapproves. You don't have to know much else, just remember that the higher powers—cops, council, parents, clergy—disapprove. My grandmother knows this and supports it.

"He's a forgiving God," she reminds me, tearing another bit off the chicken and dipping it in the congealed grease at the bottom of the pan. Grandma's a great hinter. She just knows I'm up to the most vile, perverse activities any neighborhood kid ever dreamed up, and she's waiting for me to see the light.

To her, I think, God is this force perched just above the town of Sturbridge, watching with a heavy hand, ready to strike us down if we sneak a beer by the river or touch a willing girlfriend below the neck. Somehow he gets his word across through the pale Reverend Fletcher, who grips my hand with a giant smile every Sunday—as if everything's forgotten—and says he hopes I'll be at the youth group meeting that night. I won't be.

Grandma heads back to the living room. I cover the chicken with the foil and shove it into the refrigerator.

Al's already dressed for practice when I get to the gym Monday, sitting on the bench by our lockers. "He wants to see us," he says, pointing to the coach's office. So we go in and sit down, and Coach has what I'd call his understanding frown on. Like he's disappointed in us about something, but he's ready to talk man to man.

"I heard you guys had a fight?" He's looking at me.

I shake my head kind of slowly. "No."

He looks at Al.

Al lowers his chin and raises his eyebrows. "No."

"Were you guys drinking Saturday night?"

"Just Pepsi," Al says.

Coach looks at me again. "No way," I say. We're all quiet for about twenty seconds. "There was no fight."

"That's not how I heard it."

"I wouldn't fight this guy," Al says. "No way. We just worked some on takedowns. We were psyched up."

Coach says, "Mm-hmm."

He looks at me. I say that's all it was.

"Al, you can go," he says.

Al shuts the door and Coach still has that look on, a little more intense maybe. "I know this is tough on you, Benny," he says.

"What is?"

"I'm the one who told Hatcher to cut to 140," he says. "I made Al stay at 135. It's real nice that they wanted to make room for you, but this isn't about being buddies." He picks up a pen from the desk and starts clicking it on and off, keeping his eyes right on mine. "The both of those guys could win state titles this year. You know how incredible that would be? They need every advantage they can get, and they're staying at those weight classes."

"I know." I don't get this lecture at all.

"I know you don't like it," he says. "But I better not hear about you taking any cheap shots at Al."

Now I get it. He's got to be kidding. "I never took a cheap shot at anybody."

"That's not how I heard it." His favorite phrase.

He heard wrong, but I can't say that to him. I just stare at him until he tells me to get ready for practice.

I'm numb for the rest of the day.

My grandmother comes over again on Wednesdays, but she doesn't stay long. She and my mother, sometimes my father, go to the weekly covered-dish supper at the church. Eighteen different varieties of macaroni and cheese. And as an added bonus, the Reverend Fletcher offers a delightful and informative talk on how evil and sinful we all are, just in case the message didn't get through on Sunday.

I walk into the kitchen as they're getting ready to go. My mom is looking for her oven mitt to get the casserole out, and I catch Grandma saying, "He sure is a patient God." Just about anything my mother or anybody else might have said could have triggered that response.

"Won't you join us, Benjy?" Mom says.

"I don't think so," I say. "The movie's at eight. I think I'll shave."

I'm taking Kim to the movies over in Weston. I asked her yesterday afternoon before practice, and she didn't hesitate or anything.

"You're going to a movie on a school night?" Grandma asks, as if it's any of her business.

"It's a date, Grandma," I say. I turn to my mother. "Dad going?"

"He hasn't come in yet," she says, "so I doubt it. They're very busy at work for some reason. Let me get you some of this," she says as she lifts the stuff out of the oven.

"Nah. I'm gonna stop at McDonald's with Kim."

"Kim what?" Grandma wants to know.

"Chavez," I say very clearly, knowing it will spoil her week.

"Sounds Catholic," she says matter-of-factly.

"Sounds even worse than that, doesn't it?"

Grandma doesn't mind the few black people in the area, but if you're Catholic and/or Puerto Rican, you'd better keep out of her way. I guess she figures that as long as her God is patient and wise and forgiving, she doesn't have to be.

"Watch it, Ben," Mom says, but she isn't much more tolerant of Grandma than I am. Mom's tough; she's a nurse part-time at the hospital, and she stays in shape with jogging and cycling and stuff. She used to work at Hatcher's dad's office, but she walked out on him last summer. I never did figure out why.

"I'll drive you down," I say. It's only a few blocks, but she's got the dinner to carry and it's pretty cold out.

I back out the driveway, and Dad's walking up the hill so I stop for a minute. Mom rolls down her window and he comes over and kisses her.

"We'll be back about eight," she says. "There's food in the oven."

"I'm just dropping them off," I say to him. "I'll be right back."

When I get back, he's at the kitchen table in his undershirt with a beer and the plate from the oven. He's picking at his teeth with his index finger. "What's with you?" he says.

I shrug. "Got a date tonight."

He nods approvingly. "Somebody I know?"

"I dunno. Kim Chavez. She's a junior."

"Oh. . . . How'd practice go?"

"Not bad." It wasn't. "I'm gettin' there." I am. I'm not sure where I'm getting to, but I'm holding my own, even with Al at times. "You guys are busy, huh?"

"Yeah. Some big deal went through." He takes a swig of the beer, finishing it. He needs a shave a heck of a lot more than I do, even though it's only been twelve hours. Last time I shaved was Saturday.

"Where you going?"

"Movies."

I open the refrigerator and get a glass of milk, and hand him another bottle of Schaefer. He was out last night, doing one of his jobs, I think. "We got a scrimmage on Saturday," I say.

"I know. I'll be there."

McDonald's is crowded, and we get on the line nearest the door. There's a skinny old lady in a violet kerchief and a big heavy coat standing to the side, looking flustered. "Speak *up*, Harold," she says to a guy, her husband, who's at the counter trying to get somebody's attention; needing ketchup or something else they forgot. "He just stands there," she says to me, shaking her head. "He stands there and they ignore him. . . . Speak *up*, Harold."

Kim meets my eyes with a smile. She's got on a white-and-pink striped button-down shirt, with designer jeans and running shoes. The silver chain's there, too. We're third on line, and I catch Chrissy Lane's eye behind the counter and wave with two fingers. I motion toward

Harold with my head, and Chrissy looks over at him attentively. She smiles and reaches under the counter for McNugget sauce, and he thanks her and moves away.

We get our food and head for a booth. A little kid in a purple YMCA SOCCER T-shirt comes racing around the corner and I have to juggle the tray to keep from dumping it. Kim grabs my arm and she feels pretty strong for such a little thing. Some guys from the basketball team are at one of the booths, and I nod in greeting and sit with my back to them.

She eats a lot, so we don't talk too much during dinner. "You know that guy in the Syracuse sweatshirt?" I ask, referring to one of the guys at the basketball table.

"Yeah?"

"I heard his brother deals coke."

"Yeah. I've heard that," she says. "People jump to conclusions. It's not true."

"No?"

She shakes her head. "Some of his friends. Danny's okay."

Kim's only lived here about two years, but she knows more about certain aspects of the town than I do. She knows who's getting what from who, and who's into drugs and anorexia and things like that. I offer her a french fry because she's already finished hers. She takes it.

I tell her what the coach said on Monday, and she frowns and clicks her tongue. "That's really unfair," she says. "I had a teacher like that in seventh grade. She couldn't stand me and made my life miserable. She gave me C's and B's until my parents went to the principal about it."

"Yeah, well, I don't think Coach is down on me, particularly. He's just protecting Al. He hasn't coached a state champ yet, and he thinks I'm a threat to that."

"Sounds real mature." She's smiling when she says this; she seems to have some understanding of this rutting behavior we males go through. Most girls seem to be repelled by it; Kim just seems amused. "I guess Coach is about as grown-up as you guys are," she says. "He'd probably jump you in the backyard too." We both laugh at this, but I think it's got some truth to it.

"So . . . are you?" she asks.

"What?"

"A threat. To Al."

"I don't know." I don't. I ought to be. But I'm not really sure.

"He's the best in the state?" she asks.

"Yeah. . . . He could probably win at any weight from 130 to 140."

"Can you beat him?"

I think about this for half a minute, then I answer yes. "I have to."

She folds her arms. "Why?"

"It's what I am."

"What is?"

"A wrestler. From Sturbridge. I'm a kid from Sturbridge."

"That's why you have to beat Al?"

I don't know. "I think so."

"I'm a kid from Sturbridge," she says. Her voice is gentle, but firm. "I want to win a state title, too. I plan to. But for me."

"Yeah." I bite down on my lip. I haven't talked this much to a girl in my life. "I don't mean nothing bad by this, but . . . you're not really from here. Not like I am."

"I know," she says. "But you don't have a chain around your leg, either. I like it here, Ben. But this is a pretty small pond."

She brings her fist down gently on my hand, then grabs her purse and gets up to go to the bathroom. I turn as inconspicuously as I can to watch her walk away, and I see that the basketball players are watching her, too. One of them—Damon Henderson, the point guard—gives me a sly smile. He waits a few seconds to make sure she's out of earshot, then he points toward the bathroom door and gives me a raised-fist salute. I laugh, a little embarrassed but glad to have been seen with her.

She takes my arm on the way out and I can smell her toothpaste. I'm feeling pretty good about things. I go around and open the car door for her, then pull out to Route 6. We're turning left, but I look the other way to check traffic and of course I can see the Mobil station up there. I'm torn for just a second, maybe even guilty, but I don't even know that girl's name.

Kim slides toward me just a little to turn on the radio, but then she stays there after it comes on.

I think I'm falling in love, but I'm not sure with who. Maybe just with the idea of it all.

Guys I'm certain my mother has
slept with:

  * my father

Guys I'm not sure about:

  * somebody back in high school

  * Hatcher's dad

December

You can't help but be electrified by the noise, though I'm trying hard not to be. The varsity guys burst out of the locker room and start circling the mat, and everybody in the stands is on their feet chanting "Stur-*bridge*" (stamp, stamp), "Stur-*bridge*."

I start rubbing my shoulder—it really doesn't hurt anymore, but I'm feeling conspicuous, embarrassed to be sitting here in regular clothes in a folding chair next to the assistant coach. Al is jumping up and down out there, shoving Hatcher playfully, then making a fist toward the stands.

The pep band is playing "On Wisconsin," here in Pennsylvania, and there isn't an empty seat in the whole gym. My father's up there, and Kim is up on the very top row with her girlfriends. The guys from Weston South are warming up on the side of the gym, looking around and probably feeling intimidated. Nobody's come in here and beat us in nine years.

The bleachers are speckled with shiny blue Sturbridge Wrestling Boosters Association jackets. Anybody who actually wrestled has his graduation year and nickname stitched on the chest: "Spins '83"; "Bucky '78." Some of them even carry old clippings from the *Sturbridge Observer* in their wallets to settle arguments. Everybody's got a hat on, too. I'm the only guy in town who doesn't wear an advertisement for a bar, a tractor, a sports team, or a cigarette on his head.

There's one rather large person in the front row with a jacket labeled "Mom," which I'm sure she thinks is cute. But it's actually useful information, because otherwise it'd be hard to tell if she's a man, a woman, or a Bulgarian shot-putter.

Hatcher's father is walking out to the mat with a microphone for the announcements. They do this every year at the first match—the booster club president introduces the local dignitaries, who are always the same: Peter Valdez and Jerry Franken, the town's state champions; Mayor Andrew Watt ("Who?" we all say. "No, Watt."); the principal; the wrestling coaches; the captains (Al and Hatcher).

I catch Al's father looking at me and I nod. He gives me a thumbs-up signal. The band starts playing their other song ("Louie, Louie") and little Anthony Terranova—our man at 103—starts putting on his headgear and talking to the coach.

Anthony races onto the mat—he's a sophomore but just barely beat Tommy Austin in their wrestle-off two days ago. (Al beat me 9–2 in ours.) He takes down the guy from South in about four seconds, and has him on his back right away. He's got him cradled and he's driving hard with his legs. The ref slams the mat for a pin, and the place erupts as the first match of the season ends in twenty-eight seconds.

Al and Digit leap off the bench and start hugging Anthony, and he goes down the line slapping five with everybody. The "Stur-*bridge*" chant starts again, and the music, and somebody tosses a roll of toilet paper onto the mat, which is another one of the traditions. It unravels maybe forty sheets and comes to a stop at the edge of the mat. The referee picks it up and carries it over to our coach, who grins and sends the next wrestler out.

By the time Digit gets out there we're up 15–3, and it gets better. He and his opponent circle around each other for about thirty seconds, then Digit shoots in and flips the guy and it's over almost before you realize it.

Digit puts a towel around his neck, picks up a squirt bottle, and sits next to me. He yells the whole time while Al and Hatcher pin their guys in the first period, then sits back and watches the rest of the match. We wind up winning 54–9.

People pour out of the stands onto the mat, and the guys who wrestled start working their way toward the locker room. I just stand there, looking around and looking dumb. Al's father wanders up to me and grabs my arm. "Nice job out there tonight," he says to me, and I don't think he's being sarcastic.

"Thanks," I say. "I mean, they did really good."

"You kicked their asses," he says, looking around, probably for Al. He's skinny, with kind of long hair for a guy as old as he is, and it's curly and dark with streaks of gray. He sticks a finger in his ear and starts scratching with it. It's just the two of them; Al's mother died a couple of years ago. Cancer. Al's got an older brother in the army who I haven't seen in a long time.

Kim waves at me from over by the exit, and I put up two

fingers like a wave. I start walking toward the locker room. Tommy Austin is standing under the basket talking to three girls who wouldn't normally have given him the time of day. But he's wrestling JV and pinned his opponent, and everybody figures he'll be varsity pretty soon. We've already stopped calling him Susan.

Tim Royce—171 two years ago—sticks out his hand to me and I shake it. "You hurt?" he asks.

"Nah."

"What's up?"

I shrug. "Kind of a bottleneck. I'm odd man out right now."

"Too bad." He starts rubbing his chin. His T-shirt says PENN STATE ATHLETIC DEPARTMENT, but he goes to Weston Community College. And he's obviously not wrestling there, as he's up to at least 200 pounds. "Get tougher," he says.

"Yeah. See ya around."

I reach the door to the lockers, but I don't have any reason to go in. Kim's talking to one of her friends, but I know she's waiting for me, even though we didn't make any plans or anything.

I duck into the door and head down the stairs to the locker room, which is already thick with steam. Music is blaring and guys are whooping it up. Coach spots me and he's all smiles. "Ben-jee," he says. "Benny-man. Great show tonight, huh?"

"Fantastic," I say, but my voice is flat.

"Best team this school ever had," he says, which may be so, but they've got an awful lot to prove first. Coach turns into his office and I head for the exit.

Al's by his locker, naked, with one foot up on the bench,

and he's drying between his toes with a towel. "Hey," he says.

"Hey," I say back. "Your old man was looking for you."

"Oh, yeah? He still upstairs?"

"I think so."

"Would you tell him I'll be right up? I'll meet him outside."

"Sure."

Hatcher's standing there half-dressed, staring at Al. "You're going home with your father?" he says, as if it's the most unbelievable thing he's ever heard.

"Yeah," Al says. "I had to cut weight today, remember? I ain't eaten anything since six o'clock this morning. He probably hasn't either."

"I thought we were gonna hang out," Hatcher says.

"Guess not," Al says, drying his armpits as he walks away from Hatcher. Hatcher looks after him with a screwed-up frown, then yells over to Digit to see if he's up for hanging out.

I go upstairs and tell Al's father he's coming, then finally get out of there.

In the parking lot I bump into Jerry Franken, which really sucks because I'm trying to get away from this. He puts a beefy arm around me, and I can tell he had garlic for dinner.

"That Al is something, huh?" he says to me.

"Sure is."

"Must be tough to watch."

I start nodding my head. "It is."

"Can't you move up?"

I've been through this a thousand times—with my father, with some of the teachers, with my non-wrestling friends.

"It'd be a big jump in weight, up or down," I say.

"Yeah," he says. "You got two, three really tough people there."

"Yeah, we do."

He shakes his head. "Just hang in there. You need a ride?"

"Nah. I wanna walk." I do. I could have gotten a ride from Al or Kim or my father or just about anybody, but I want to walk. I want to get out of here. I want to think about winning the state championship. About destroying Al.

"See ya," I say, and start crossing the lawn. Franken's okay. He puts on wrestling clinics for the elementary school kids every year, which is how I first got into the sport.

The school is down my end of town, but it's on the other side of Main, a block up from the plant. I start walking up toward the other end—the end where the hospital is and the Turkey Hill store, but I stay on Maple Street, the block parallel to Main. It's dark and quiet. I'm not going anywhere in particular. Just away from that bullshit behind me.

Maple is above Main as you climb the hill on this side, so you can look down on the stores and stuff. Sturbridge is almost like a stadium—there's a flat two-block-wide valley down the spine of the town, then it rises up on both sides. It's a pit only the strongest crawl out of.

I live on the hill on the other side from where I'm walking, across the Pocono River. Most of the homes are on the hills, with six blocks of stores and stone churches and a couple of bars on the flats. The traffic lights on either end define the business section.

On the one end of town, behind me as I'm walking, is Route 6. Up beyond the other light you cross the river again—it sort of snakes around the town—and Main becomes North Main, a section of bigger houses and bigger yards, some doctors and lawyers and families that go way back. Hatcher lives out there.

Kim lives out that way, too. Both of her parents are elementary school teachers over in Weston, and they coach the swimming teams at North.

It's a decent night—52 degrees at 9:48. Kids who were at the match are already gathered down on Main. Rite Aid is still open—they do a good business in the half hour after a match.

I walk into Turkey Hill, past the magazine rack and down the cupcake and potato chip aisle, toward the refrigerated section in the back. I stare through the glass door at the drinks: bottles of Hawaiian Punch and Pepsi and Gatorade, cartons of iced tea and milk, cans of Coke and 7-Up. After about a minute I take out a carton of orange drink and walk back toward the register, shaking the carton as I go.

I have to wait behind a fat girl about twelve buying *Seventeen* magazine and a bag of popcorn, and a guy about forty with glasses and a tie on carrying a giant Styrofoam cup of coffee, *The New York Times*, a box of chocolate doughnut gems, and a copy of *Penthouse*. He has exact change, but it takes him a while to dig it out. I grab a straw and finish the orange drink before I even pay for it.

Kim drives past as I come out of the store, but she isn't looking this way. Digit is in the passenger seat, and I can interpret that several ways. I head toward Court Street, because they'll be coming back along Main any minute.

Court runs parallel to Main on the other side, hugging the river most of the way.

I have this dumb idea of where I'm headed, and I let myself think it's because I'm still thirsty. The river moves faster along here; the drop in elevation isn't great, but it's enough to cause some rapids. So it's a different town here, just two blocks in from Main, and it's dark and quiet and sleepy.

Sometimes late at night I run through here, past the houses and the courthouse and the jail. The town's fast asleep between one-thirty and six, and you can run through like you're in another dimension.

I start walking a little faster when I reach Route 6, since I'm out in the open now. I just don't feel like seeing anybody connected with the wrestling team or the school. Or the whole town. I'll deal with them all later.

What is it with Kim anyway? I think she's got her head together too much for me to handle. She makes me want to find answers about myself, but I don't even know the right questions.

I've had one girlfriend to speak of in my life. We started hanging around together the summer before our junior year, and started making out one night in August. Noreen Califano. I can't even look her in the face anymore.

I was shy. I didn't really feel comfortable being with her except in private. Our dates were football games that fall, and after the third one I told her I didn't think it was working out.

Two weeks later I started calling her on the phone again.

I'd see her in school and she'd ignore me, but I'd call her as soon as I got home. And she'd be polite as can be, and sometimes we even had some decent conversations. And finally I asked her to go to the movies. She'd have to drive because I didn't have my license yet. She said okay.

The next day she said forget it. Her friends told her I was using her because she could drive. And no way should she lower herself after I dumped her for no reason.

I kept calling. She kept being okay to me on the phone.

Then the year's first edition of *The Lions' Roar* came out. That's the school paper. I read the very first line in the gossip column, for all the world to see: Urgent message from NC to Big Ben—"Leave me *alone!*"

I laugh about it now. Ha, ha.

I reach the Mobil station, and the girl is inside the office, talking on the phone. The older guy is at the pumps.

I stick my hand in my pocket to keep all the change from rattling, and go up to the door and look inside. She puts her hand over the phone and looks up and says "Yeah?"

"Could I get some change?" I say, waving a dollar.

She opens a drawer and takes out four quarters, handing them to me and taking the dollar. The guy outside yells "Jody," and I see that there's three cars waiting for service. She says "I gotta go" into the phone and hangs up.

The vending machines are off to the side by the diesel pumps in an open, rectangular aluminum shed: three drink machines (Coke, Pepsi, and juices) and a food one with candy, pretzels, and stuff like that. I get a can of orange soda and a package of six Oreo cookies. Then I leave, because the girl is busy and looks too beautiful for me.

My father is not waiting up; my mother is home from work. I climb the stairs and hear them talking softly in their bedroom. Their door is closed and the light is off.

I close my door and lie in the dark on my own bed. It occurs to me that Digit and Kim may still be out driving around, or worse. I kick off my shoes. I am empty.

What I might be doing in a year:

  * wrestling at Penn State (right)

  * wrestling at Weston CC

  * wrestling with my sanity

What I definitely won't be doing:

  * working at the plant

  * enlisting in the army

  * joining the boosters association

I get a pass to the library on Monday out of study hall and pull out the yearbooks from the past few years. I finally find her in the graduating class of two years ago: Jody Mullins. I think I remember her vaguely, but not the way I see her now.

In the yearbook photo she looks different, repressed. Her hair is short, not flowing and full like it is now, and her face is rigid and squinty. Under Activities she's got Band 1, 2; Tennis 1; Distributive Education 4. There's no nickname listed.

I flip to the section of candid photos and search in vain for another shot of her. I think I see the side of her head in a picture from the senior awards luncheon, but that doesn't tell me much except that she might have been there.

I'd hoped to discover that she was a wrestling groupie all grown-up, who still held some secret unfulfilled desires that maybe I could help with. But I haven't seen her anywhere except the Mobil station, and I don't know if she's ever even been to a wrestling match.

I take the long way back to study hall so I can pass Kim's history class. I hang outside the door until I catch her eye, and she looks a little tentative but gives a smile and a tiny, hesitant wave.

I get back to study hall and sit next to Digit, who's reading *Sports Illustrated*.

"We going to Hatcher's tonight?" I ask.

"Yeah, I guess." We watch Monday night football there most weeks. "Run yesterday?" he says.

"About four miles."

"Me and Al did three." He closes the magazine and yawns. "Where'd you go after the match Saturday?"

"Home. Where'd you go?"

"Just hung around," he says.

"You do anything?"

"Drove around."

He's not saying much. So I get more direct. "You put any moves on her?"

Digit raises his eyebrows and sits up straighter. He says "No" with no emphasis at all.

"Oh."

"Why would I?" he asks, a little sharper.

"Why wouldn't you?"

He laughs. "Who do you think she was looking for all night?"

I shrug, but that means I know.

"She thought I was trying to help her find you, but I knew where you were the whole time. I kept telling her where to turn so we'd be sure to miss you."

"How come?"

"You obviously didn't want to get found."

I nod my head. "So what'd she say?"

"She said she doesn't mind a chase if there's some chance of catching up. But she doesn't know what you're running from." He starts picking at a scab on his jaw where he cut off a zit shaving. He doesn't have much experience with a razor. "I don't know, either," he says.

I cross my arms and look at the ceiling a minute. Then I look back at Digit. "I'm too distracted, man." He looks at me like he doesn't know what I'm talking about, but I think he does. It's because of wrestling. "My whole life has built up to this season, and it might not ever happen," I say. "This is our year. My year. There's no more chances after this one."

He stares right at me. "Yeah. So?"

"I can't think about anything else right now. If I'm ever going to be anybody, it has to start this season." Digit knows this. We used to talk about it constantly. All four of us did. We'd imagine what it would be like to win the states, to be the best in Pennsylvania. Now it's staring us in the face and it's scary. And it's worse for me because I might not even get the chance. "I've never done anything worth a damn yet, Digit."

He keeps staring at me a few seconds. Then he grins. "You won that spelling bee in fourth grade."

I laugh, so he does, too. "You guys at least have the chance," I say, getting serious again. "If none of us ever does anything worth a shit, at least you guys will have something to hold on to."

"True."

I'm generally not a bitcher. Digit's the only one I've said this to; I haven't even been facing it myself. But I guess I'm more desperate than I realized.

He says one more thing. "Don't blame Coach. This is about being the best, right? Al and Hatch are best where they are. If you want your chance, you have to take it. You have to beat one of us to get it."

The bell rings to change classes, and we start walking toward the hall. "So you ain't gonna move on her?" I ask again.

"Only if you ain't gonna," he says.

On Saturday night the pep band debuts a song in Al's honor ("You Can Call Me Al" by Paul Simon). They break into it as soon as Digit's match ends and strike it up again the second Al executes his pin. This is the third match of the season and nobody's lasted a full minute with him yet.

Al does a kind of Michael Jackson moonwalk back to the bench, playing to the crowd and the band. The kid from Preston barely knew what hit him; Al had him on his back within three seconds and could have pinned him in less than ten. But Al likes to play with his food, so he pushed the guy around for forty seconds before flattening him. The crowd was on its feet the whole time, yelling for blood, or at least pain.

I take a deep breath and snap my headgear under my chin. Hatcher's moved up to 145 to get a better workout, so I'm finally out there for real at 140. I don't know when I'll get another opportunity, so I'm going to make this count.

The guy I'm wrestling outweighs me by five pounds and has longer arms and legs. He's dark, and hairier than most high school kids, and looks like he's got some anger. But I'm from Sturbridge, and second-string Sturbridge is better than most first teams. *Keystone Wrestling News* has us ranked fourth in the state. I'll kill this guy.

I have no quarrel with the smell of perspiration if it's clean: fresh and salty. But this guy stinks. He shoots in immediately, and I dodge him easily and spring away. He shoots again, and this time I slip on the spot where Al just pinned his guy. So I'm down and he's got me, and I'm two points behind and in some trouble.

He's got leverage, but not much, and I inch my way toward the edge of the mat. I'm not going to force my way out of this hold, so I need to get out of bounds. I'm used to this; Al gets me locked up uncountable times a day in practice, and I can usually keep myself from getting pinned, if not embarrassed.

It takes most of the period, but I get to the edge of the mat and let him roll me to my back, out of bounds. The ref blows his whistle and my opponent says "Shit." He gets up and walks swiftly back to the center circle. I straighten my headgear and get down on all fours below him.

I'm on my feet the instant the whistle blows, trying to force his hands apart where they're gripped around my waist. He lifts me to my feet and tries to throw me down, but I shift at just the right second and get free for an escape point. I pivot to face him, and he's already attacking. No letting up by this guy.

We've got each other by the shoulders, circling around like grizzly bears in combat, and he's slippery and exhaling in short, angry bursts. He lunges at me a couple of times, but I get out of the way.

Between periods the coach tells me to get my ass in gear and attack this guy instead of waiting for him to make all the moves. Al puts his arm on my shoulder and says, "This guy sucks. You should be killing him."

I start the second period up, but the guy is strong and I can't just muscle him to the mat. It takes me a while to finally take him down, and he escapes right away and gets to his feet. So it's 3–3, and we're back in our dancing bear routine. The second period ends that way.

The crowd is getting impatient—we won the first six weight classes by pin—and I hear some frustration as I walk back to the bench. Coach tells me to attack this guy, to get more aggressive and stop playing around. Al puts both hands on my shoulders this time and says, "This guy really sucks. You should be killing him."

I start the third period down, and if I let him exploit that, he'll just ride me the rest of the match. He already has more than a minute of riding time on me, and if we end in a draw the riding-time edge would break the tie. The guy has one move, and I should be kicking his butt. But I think I've forgotten how to win. All this time I've been learning not to lose—or at least not to get pinned—and my offense has gone to hell.

I rocket to my feet and break away pretty easily, and I can tell this guy is getting exhausted. I shoot in and take him down hard, and I hear the wind go out of him as he hits the mat.

He's the one in trouble now, and he lets out an "nnn-nnn-nnn" sound as I force his shoulders toward the mat. He'll either get pinned or his arm will break, and after a few seconds of struggle I feel him let go.

The ref slams the mat with his palm and I get to my knees. I let out my breath and the ref lifts my arm, and I walk off the mat and slap hands with Digit.

Coach shows me his fist and shakes it approvingly. Al pats my head and says, "That guy sucked. What took you so long?"

Things I've done twice:

  * pinned Al (seventh grade)

  * told my father to go to hell

  * read *Conditioning for Wrestling:
    The Iowa Way*

Things I haven't:

  * left home for four days

  * been suspended from school for
    telling a teacher to kiss my ass

  * had sex

Our program doesn't have the type of budget some of these top-ranked schools have, sending their teams to tournaments in Las Vegas and Chicago and Iowa. The biggest deal we get is an overnight trip to Allentown for the Lehigh Valley Holiday Invitational. Of the eight teams there, three of us are ranked nationally.

Coach lets me go along, even though I'm not wrestling, and we win the title by two points over Phillipsburg, New Jersey, which *USA Today* has at number six. Digit loses his first match of the season in the final to a kid from Maryland, but Al stays unbeaten by pinning a guy from Bethlehem on the day before Christmas. Hatcher wins, too.

We also finish ahead of Northampton, which according to *Keystone Wrestling News* was the best team in Pennsylvania. Not any longer.

We sneak a few beers in the back of the bus on the way home from the tournament. Coach sits up front and brags to the bus driver about what a great team we have. It's only his fourth season here, and he figures he's got a lot to live up to.

Digit spends most of the time staring out the window. He led going into the final period, but got taken down twice in the last minute. He says he learned something. I think he's the most likely of us all to win a state title this year, because he's so intense. We still hang out most nights, but he heads home by nine. Me and Al and Hatcher usually sit on Main Street at least until Rite Aid closes. But Digit's drifting off. Even after a match he doesn't quite let go—he keeps running it over in his mind. So he's even more distant today, since he lost. He's not mooning anybody like Al and Hatcher and some of the others are.

When our heavyweight, Billy Avery, presses his bare butt against the glass, it covers the whole window. We all crack up at that. Digit opens another beer. Hatcher takes a red pixie football out of his gym bag and tosses it at Billy, but it misses by two feet and hits Anthony Terranova in the head. Anthony throws the football back at Hatcher, who grabs it and whips it back. This time it hits Billy, who starts pulling up his pants in a hurry.

By the time we turn off the turnpike by Scranton, there's one cracked window, a pool of beer on the floor, and a couple of ripped seat cushions. Coach yells back at us to shut up for a while. Al starts singing "Downtown Train," and Digit joins in.

I go with Mom and Dad and Grandma to the 5:00 P.M. service on Christmas day. I stopped at Kim's house for a few minutes just before. She gave me a tape of her psych-up music. I got her a ceramic whale.

So we're driving to the church and Mom asks me about her. "I guess you two really like each other?" she says.

"I guess." I'm not exactly sure. I mean I like her fine, but nothing seems to be happening.

"Seems like a nice girl," says Dad, who met her after the last home match.

Grandma snorts. "I hope she knows how to keep her legs crossed," she says, just oozing with Christmas spirit.

Me and Mom and Dad just look at each other and roll our eyes. We've reached the church. Jerry Franken and his wife are the greeters. His wife winks at me and smiles a big toothy smile. Jerry gives me a light punch on the arm. "We knocked off some big boys yesterday, huh?"

"We're number one," I say, kind of ironically, I think. It's hard to be bothered by this guy.

"See you Tuesday?" he asks.

"Sure." School's closed this week. We're putting on a clinic at the Y for little kids.

We sit in a pew and wait. I check my watch and it says 5:06, and I can see we're in for high comedy again. Reverend Fletcher and the wimpy youth minister, Paul Long, will show up in about three minutes, bursting through the doors singing "Joy to the World" at the top of their lungs. They'll be just so surprised to see the church full of people, having completely forgotten that they'd scheduled a service for this afternoon. "We were out caroling," Fletcher will say, removing a red-and-white striped scarf.

"Did we schedule a service?" Paul will say, looking at a little girl in the front row. She'll laugh and say yes. He'll turn to the Reverend in surprise, and they'll say in spontaneous unison, "Well, then let's have a service."

Maybe you can sense that they've done this before.

I hear them coming up the steps. They're singing "Hark the Herald Angels . . ."

Get me out of here.

Things that I've mastered:

    * talking to myself

    * staring down an opponent

    * not getting pinned

Things I can't even do:

    * fly a kite

    * read music

    * figure out what girls are thinking

I walk down the hill to Al's house late Tuesday morning, crossing the footbridge over the river. The clinic's at noon. Al's father answers the door and I step into the living room. I haven't been here in about a month; there's too much unspoken tension between me and Al. If Digit's around, it's easy to avoid, but one-on-one it's almost impossible to ignore. Al has something I have to get, and there's no way to share it even if we would.

I can see him in the kitchen, on the phone. His father points to the couch and tells me to sit down. He's wearing old stained work pants and a sleeveless white T-shirt.

"He's talking to Joe," he says. Al's brother. I think he's stationed in Texas.

"You off today?" I ask.

"Yeah." He stretches out his left arm and yawns. "I always take a day or two after Christmas. Coke or something? Orange juice?"

"I just ate. But thanks."

He straightens out some newspapers on the coffee table. He's got a cigarette smoldering in an ashtray on the table, too, but it looks like he forgot about it. The ash is about two inches long.

"Dad." Al's standing in the doorway with the phone. His father comes over and takes it, and goes into the kitchen.

"Hey," Al says to me.

"Hey. You ready?"

"Need my jacket."

I follow him into the kitchen. His old man is laughing into the phone. "Never a dull moment," he's saying. Al points to the kitchen table, where there's a package of salami and some crackers. "You hungry?" he asks me.

"No thanks."

Al grabs his father's shoulder and says he'll be back for dinner. "Tell Joe I'll talk to him again soon."

We head down the walk and Al pulls his gloves out of his pocket and puts them on. He looks over his shoulder at the house as we cross Court Street. "My mom died two years ago," he says.

"Two years today?"

"Yeah. It's real hard on him. But he's doing okay."

"He seemed okay. That's why your brother called?"

"Pretty much. We try to stay close."

"Yeah."

We walk in silence for a few blocks. We have to cross back over the river to get to the Y, which is down the other end of town.

"Lot of kids signed up?" Al says.

"I heard about fifty." That's a lot of kids for the Y's small gym, but we'll squeeze them in. It's first, second, and third graders today. The older kids get their turn on Thursday.

The gym is old—it used to be an armory, and if you're playing basketball you can't shoot from past the top of the key without hitting a girder. But there isn't a kid in town who hasn't spent a lot of hours in there, playing hoops or indoor soccer or floor hockey.

The Y is in the far corner of town, where the river makes its right angle. We enter the gym and about twenty little kids come running over to see Al, slapping five with him or just looking at him in awe. They don't ignore me either, but Al gets most of the attention. They even want autographs.

Jerry Franken blows his whistle and tells everybody to sit in the bleachers. They hustle over, laughing and shoving, and Jerry goes over the agenda. Mostly we want them to have fun, to get a feel for the sport. Mostly they want to try and annihilate each other.

We break into groups more or less by size. I've got mostly second graders, and we go over some basic moves for about forty-five minutes. One really skinny kid named Cody keeps asking if they can do tag team matches, but I tell him that's just on TV. After a while I let him and three others wrestle me at once. I let them pin me after a couple of minutes.

I roll to my stomach and they sit on my back. I reach around and tickle the skinny kid, sticking my thumb in his armpit. Then I tell them to go get a drink, and they all race to the water fountain. I look up and Kim's standing by the entrance to the gym.

I wave and go over. She's got a big smile.

"They like you," she says.

"I like them. What are you up to?"

"I was lifting." She makes a muscle. I touch it with two fingers.

"Nice crowd," she says.

Two of the kids from my group come over. "That your girlfriend?" one of them asks.

"Your lover girl?" says the other one.

I laugh. "Go do a hundred push-ups," I say.

"Yeah, right."

They both laugh and walk back into the gym. Most of the kids from my group are out there wrestling in groups of four or five. I turn to Kim and say bye. "Take it easy out there!" I yell to the kids, running over to the mats.

I look back and Kim's still standing in the doorway. Al's group goes running for the water fountain next, and he's carrying two first graders piggyback. The kids are laughing their heads off. He gets over there and yells "Help!" to Kim. "Peel these knuckleheads off me!"

Kim takes one and Al lets the other one down. Then he flops on the floor like he's totally out of energy, and four more kids pile on top.

Franken blows his whistle and says it's time for the video, so everybody goes back to the bleachers. Franken rolls in a big-screen TV and a VCR. Somebody shuts the lights, and we watch a highlights film from the past few seasons, including Al losing last year's state semifinal in overtime.

Later we hand out T-shirts and certificates and the parents arrive to pick up their kids. The kids are all beaming and begging their parents to take them to our match on Saturday. A lot of them hug my legs, and one even kisses my hand.

When I'm ready to leave, Al is sitting in the bleachers with Franken, deep in conversation. So I just catch his eye and say "See you later." They both yell "So long," and Jerry adds "Thanks a lot."

I step out into the sun and walk up toward Main Street, feeling like I've been bombarded with affection. It isn't a bad sensation.

WHERE WE STAND

ME (135) vs. DIGIT (130): At present weights, I'd win 60 percent of the time. But dried out to 130, I'd lose 98 percent.

AL (135) vs. DIGIT (130): Al wins 95 percent. No reason for him to cut weight, or for Digit to add.

HATCHER (140) vs. DIGIT (130): Hatcher wins 98 percent. Too much weight difference.

HATCHER (140) vs. AL (135): Even giving away five pounds, Al wins 90 percent. If Hatcher cut to 135, it wouldn't even be competitive.

HATCHER (140) vs. ME (135): At present weights, Hatcher wins 90 percent. If he had a reason to cut five pounds, I'd probably win half. Gaining five pounds wouldn't do me much good, since the difference is all muscle. I don't have time to put on five useful pounds.

ME vs. AL: Stranger things have happened.

CHAPTER 10

January

Kim called me on New Year's and asked me to go to her cousin's wedding with her a week later. Why not, I figured. Seeing a transplanted New York Puerto Rican marry a Pennsylvania dairy farmer would be an experience.

So we're at the Lackawanna Station hotel in Scranton, drinking 7-Up at the bar and waiting for the reception to begin. The wedding was six hours ago, but they had to schedule things around the afternoon milking. We got lunch, saw a movie, and hung around town in between.

It's easy enough to tell which of the guests are from which family. Aaron's family is enormous (not that there's so many of them, they're just enormous individuals). One of his uncles is sitting two stools down from me, flirting with every one of Kim's female relatives that walks past. He's about sixty and wheezy, chain-smoking Camels, with a powder-blue polyester leisure suit and a pistol in a holster that he's trying to show off while looking inconspicuous. I'll assume he's in law enforcement.

The most attention he's drawn so far is from one of the Brooklyn aunts, a heavily lipsticked woman about his age who must think she's twenty-five and seems not to have realized that she's forty pounds overweight. She has a huge, lumpy cleavage and a clingy black blouse, and I'm trying hard not to look over that way.

Kim, on the other hand, looks so beautiful I could die.

We finally get into the ballroom and sit with Kim's parents, two aunts and two uncles, and an old couple that's friends on the groom's side. Kim's father gets a pitcher of beer, partly for my benefit, but I go real easy on it. Kim sips white wine.

They serve capons with stuffed potatoes and string beans. I'm sitting between Kim and her dad, so we talk about wrestling and track and swimming, and how there's a lot of similarities, being out there all by yourself with nobody to pass the ball to or run interference. You either win or you lose, and the degree to which either happens is totally dependent on you.

Her dad has a coach's demeanor, but not like my coach. This guy is lean and limber, with a dark mustache and short hair and a smile that's genuine. His wife is Kim's size and stylish.

When the band starts, I squirm a little. They open with "We've Only Just Begun," and if they stick to that tempo I'll be wishing they'd only just get finished. But they jump into "Satisfaction" and "Surfin' U.S.A.," and the dance floor fills right up. Kim starts tugging on my arm—her parents are already up and they dance pretty well; you can tell they really enjoy each other. I roll my eyes and take off my jacket. She grabs my hand and leads me out there, and I dance about as well as I can, which ain't good.

They do "Twist and Shout" and "Light My Fire," and I start working up a sweat. At the final crash of the drums we all clap, and the lead singer announces a special request. I turn to walk off when he picks up his accordion, but Kim pulls me back. "You know how to polka, don't you?" she asks.

Well, sure. I've seen it enough on TV. Somehow I don't feel like I'm dressed for it, but I find myself swinging awkwardly around the floor to an oompah beat. I should have expected this in Scranton.

I have to admit that it's fun. Not that I'll be buying any polka tapes or anything, but bouncing around with Kim and feeling silly is a tolerable thing to do on a Sunday evening. We only stumble a couple of times.

They take it down for "The Wind Beneath My Wings," and my sweat suddenly turns cold. She reaches out her arms, but I wipe my forehead and nod toward the table. We walk off, close together but not touching. Kim looks a little surprised that I wanted to stop. Slow dancing doesn't take much effort, after all.

We sit down. "Your parents dance really good," I say. They're turning slowly, pressed together and gazing into each other's eyes. I feel like people are staring at me, but no one is. I think I know how those capons must have felt. Kim seems to sense my mood change.

She gets up and says she's going to the ladies' room, and I say I'll go, too. We start walking out. "You okay?" she says.

"Yeah. Fine. . . . Why?"

She shrugs. "Nothing, I guess."

The pistol-packing guy in the powder-blue suit is at one of the urinals when I pull up. He's got a cigarette behind his ear and keeps clearing his throat. He nods in greeting.

"Good party," I say.

"Yep," he says. "Lot of nice-looking broads."

"Sure are."

"Lot of hot-blooded women." He winks at me. "Looks like you found one."

"Yeah, I guess."

"Oh, yes," he says. "A lot of hot tamales out there, if you know what I mean."

I nod as if I do. I flush with my elbow. The guy is still pissing, or at least standing there trying. "See you later," I say.

"Yep," he says. "Don't catch anything."

Kim's parents sip coffee and talk to the other couples about work and their kids and other family things. I listen in fascination, since I haven't spent much time around normal, well-adjusted adults. Kim's mom and dad sit close and he keeps rubbing her shoulder, and they tease each other and smile a lot.

The older couple—the ones who aren't from Kim's family —just got back from a month in Florida. The guy—Dutch they call him—has white hair and very ruddy skin. His wife Ruth is fatter than he is, though not by much, and amplifies everything he says with a high laugh. They raised five kids, have eighteen grandchildren, and spend half the year traveling around in their motor home to visit them. They both were born in Scranton and never left. I learned all this just by sitting there. What they didn't tell me but was obvious is that they're best friends.

My best friends are three guys who've become my main rivals in varying degrees. Al and I may survive this season as buddies, but I'm feeling the strain. I want too badly what he has, and the only way to get it is to take it away.

My hand is on Kim's knee all this time, and she's gently stroking it with her own. She laughs a lot at what Dutch and Ruth have to say, especially when they talk about their littlest grandchildren. She grips my hand tighter when the band plays "Just the Way You Are."

After the cake and the bouquet-throwing and all that, we get up to dance again. I'm tired. So is she. They play a couple of fast ones, but then they do "Color My World" and I hold her close for the very first time. She rests her head on my shoulder and shuts her eyes, and we sway back and forth and around.

I run my hand along the back of her shoulder, slowly over her scapula, and down her side to her waist, and I linger there. Her bones are thinner, her muscles are smaller but no less firm than the ones I struggle against every day in practice. Sometimes I wonder why I spend more time entwined with Al every day than I've spent in my whole life with any female. I guess because that's the easy part, the fighting, the physical stuff. You give everything you have, but it's all focused on you, all internal. You don't have to share, don't have to figure out the harder emotions, just the easier extremes. You're not trying to meld with somebody else. Not trying to get close.

I move my hand back up her side, over the shoulder and down her spine, as low as I dare. I could reach lower, and God knows I want to, but this isn't the place or the time.

Her dress is soft cotton, black, almost sweatshirt material, and clings to her fine body like a glove. She's wearing nothing under it, at least not up top. I kiss her on the tip of the ear, and she opens her eyes and smiles. She reaches up and kisses me on the mouth, then puts her head back down and hugs tighter.

The song ends. I don't know what I'm so scared of. She runs her hand up the back of my thigh as we walk toward the table. I sit down and she sits on my lap.

We came over with her parents, so of course we're driving back with them, too. They sit closer in the front seat than we do in the back, and Kim and her mother both fall asleep. So I shut my eyes and lie back and listen to the radio all the way to town. Her dad sings softly to the classic rock of WRAZ-FM. I wonder if he used to drive around with other Puerto Rican kids and find American stations to make fun of.

They drop me off and I shake Kim's father's hand, say goodnight to her mother, and give Kim (who is awake now) a very quick kiss at about the level of her eyes. Of course I am wondering what might have been if we'd driven back from Scranton alone. Or if the wedding had been in our town, in warmer weather, with the woods or the cemetery to walk home through.

I noted when we passed the bank that it was 17 degrees at 10:51. Warm summer evenings are too many months away.

I open the door. I walk up the stairs and shut my door. I take off every piece of clothing and get under my covers, and call back the feel of her muscle, the soft smell of cotton, and the tip of her ear against my mouth.

I'm shivering.

Things we hate in this town:

* summer people from New York

* disrespectful teenagers

* anti-hunters

Things we hold dear to our hearts:

* American brotherhood

* family values

* fashionable haircuts

The guy I had tonight was slow and soft; maybe a 125er with ten pounds of fat. I pinned him in forty-eight seconds. We won ten of the thirteen matches by pin, and the other three by decision. Sturbridge 69, West Pocono 0.

I sit in front of my locker for a long time, letting the music and the towel snapping and the yelling go on around me. I'm up to 3–0, but it's hard to stay sharp when you're only competing every other week. Plus, if the other team has anybody good at 135 or 140, then Al and Hatcher stay put. I only get out there against stiffs.

I wrestled off with Al two days ago, and he beat me 10–3. I fell behind early and lost my drive, but the difference between us isn't as great as people think. I'm even starting to think I could take him.

But this season is slipping away. If I'm lucky, I'll get three more dual meets, and that will be it. A career that never was, unless I can get past Al.

Digit's already dressed; I haven't even showered yet. "You coming?" he asks.

"Yeah," I say, and start taking off my uniform. "Yeah."

We're headed for McDonald's—everybody who can afford to gain a pound or two—to celebrate our new ranking. *USA Today* has us up to eighth nationally, with no other Pennsylvania schools in the top ten. *Keystone Wrestling News* will be out in three days, and we expect to be number one in the state.

I shower in a hurry, and find Hatcher and Digit and Al waiting in Al's car in the parking lot. I wasn't sure they'd still be around; our foursome seems to be slowly dissolving.

I've spent so many nights with these guys in the past six years that I could tell you everything they dream about, every girl they've ever been interested in, every time their fathers smacked them around. But I'm not sure we even know each other this season. I'm not sure I even know myself.

Ever since junior high school we've talked about winning it all. Not just as a team, but as individuals, taking the state. Every time we'd lift weights we'd be pushing each other, busting on each other and making us work.

Or we'd stand on Main Street in the evening, watching the traffic, always with wrestling on the edge of our consciousness no matter what was going on. Being on top was a fantasy, but we were working our way into it, one workout at a time.

Even last year, when these three guys were solidly on the varsity, I still was a part of it. But now I'm like a leper, watching from the outside.

"Hey, man, we're number one," Hatcher says as I get into the car.

"Looks that way," I say.

"I was pretty worried tonight, though," Al says, not at all serious. "Especially after Coach gave that pep talk."

Coach had warned us about getting big heads, about

letting down because the other team was winless. We know better than that.

"We should have lost," Digit says with a laugh. "Let the town go home crying for once."

Al giggles. "We should do that. Next week against Wharton."

"Get out," Hatcher says. "No way."

"Not lose the whole match," Digit says. "Just scare 'em. The three of us will get pinned. We'll still win the match."

"Coach would shit in his pants," Al says. He laughs. "But screw him. I'd do it if there wasn't so much at stake."

"Number one ranking," Hatcher says.

"Top ten nationally," Digit offers.

"Immortality for the rest of our lives," Al says. "And executive positions at the cinder block factory."

"Can't wait for that," Digit says.

We pull into the McDonald's lot, and it seems almost like old times. We used to bust on our town every chance we got—the cops who've got nothing better to do than clear us off the street corners; the men who labor every weekday at the plant and cap the workday at the bars, with us—a group of sweaty kids in leotards—providing their only source of pride; the ex-wrestlers who get fat and never grow up; the oppression of the churches and the schools and the parents.

For tonight we're not part of that—we can stand back and laugh at it. But there's that feeling we all share, a feeling we don't quite give voice to. A feeling that grows stronger every day.

We won't be high school wrestlers much longer. I guess we'd better enjoy it.

Sunday morning. Mom and Dad and me and Grandma slide into a pew about three-quarters of the way back, behind two old ladies in blue coats and the Stockman family: Five well-mannered blond kids, all younger than ten, and a mom and a dad who smile too much. This week's message—I can't wait—is entitled "Our Wayward Youth."

There's a blurb on the back of the bulletin labeled "The Philadelphia Story." It tells how the youth group ("decidedly *not* wayward") is planning a three-day "ministry" in Philadelphia during Easter week, under the leadership of Youth Pastor Paul Long. I see that I'm listed as one of seventeen active members of the youth group, each of whom "has a solid relationship with Jesus Christ. Praise the Lord!"

Now, I know at least half of us are far from being active, but Grandma nudges me and points to my name, beaming. She should know better than that. I just look away. The service hasn't started yet. I look back and see the Reverend in the hallway, just about ready to glide into the sanctuary, so I shove the bulletin into my pocket.

I hurry to my feet as the organist starts the prelude, and I walk out past Fletcher and Long. Fletcher notices me and seems to flinch, a defensive reflex, no doubt. They can think I'm on my way to the bathroom, but I'm leaving for real.

Just a lost, wayward youth checking out.

I will never, ever return. Not in a million, trillion years.
Praise the Lord, I'm finished.
On Wisconsin.
We've only just begun.
I am out of here.

ORDER OF WORSHIP
9:15 A.M., January 22

ORGAN PRELUDE

CALL TO WORSHIP

> PASTOR: Let us place ourselves in His presence.

> RESPONSE: Let us be at peace.

> PASTOR: Let us halt the churning of our desires.

> RESPONSE: Let us empty all our cares.

> PASTOR: When we stop our internal fighting, then
> the healing will begin.

Kim's taking me out tonight—she asked and she paid. She picked me up in her mom's car after practice and we ate at McDonald's. Now she wants to play pool over at The Fun Zone.

It's never crowded in here this early in the evening—just some little kids with their parents burning off dinner at Skee-Ball or video games. We get a table and rack up the balls, and I break but don't sink anything. Kim walks completely around the table twice, looking for a shot, and I hold my cue kind of perpendicular to the floor and lean on it. You get to see girls from interesting angles when they're lining up a pool shot, and Kim is among the most interesting I've seen. She's got on a soft black polo shirt, slightly oversized, with PASSAIC TRACK stitched in red on the left chest.

She finally shoots, easing the three ball into a side pocket from a pretty tough line. She's got her tongue between her teeth as she lowers her head to table level, searching for her next shot. Then she comes to my side and stretches out across the table, and I'm starting to get some ideas that have nothing to do with pool.

She misses, and I chalk up my cue and make a real solid stroke that sends about ten of the balls flying but doesn't sink any.

Kim squeezes past me and she smells sweet. "'Scuse me," she says. I've got my eyes fixed on her, but I guess they stray because I look up and notice the girl—Jody, the one from the

Mobil station—sitting over to the side with another girl about her age. They've got a little kid with them, probably not even two years old, and he's playing on the floor at their feet. Jody keeps looking over at the entrance.

After a few minutes three guys come in and she stands up. The one guy, who looks vaguely familiar, is maybe three years older than me and has longish hair and a cap that says Marlboro on it. He's about my size and has a thin, fuzzy mustache.

He sees them and walks over and nods with a trace of a scowl. The other two guys leave. The Mobil girl hands the guy the baby, and says, maybe to both of them, "Long time no see."

The guy holds the kid up and says "Hey, buddy," sort of wiggling him while the kid's legs dangle. The baby looks back at Jody, reaching for her.

"It's okay," she says gently, taking the kid's finger. "That's your daddy."

I'm trying not to watch too closely, glancing around, looking at the pool table, but I'm hanging on every word. Jody is keeping an even tone, but there's enough of an edge to her voice that you could imagine her tacking "you son of a bitch" onto the end of every sentence.

"I left a message on your machine last night," she says. "Why didn't you call?"

He just says, "I was out," not looking at her.

"Daniel and I are leaving at eight," she says. "You said you'd be here at six."

"So what is it now, ten after?" he says.

"It's quarter to seven," she says. "We're leaving at eight."

She turns to her girlfriend and they start out the door. Then she stops and comes back to kiss the baby, who's starting to whine. "It's okay. You spend a little time with your daddy." She shoots a look at the guy. "We'll be over there in the pizza place. Watching."

The guy puts the kid down and takes his hand, and they walk over to the side where they've got rides for little kids. He lifts him into a rocket ship and feeds it a quarter, and it rocks back and forth while the kid spins the steering wheel.

Kim pokes me on the arm with her cue. "You know those people?" I shake my head and look at the table. I've got stripes, and all seven of them are still sitting there. There's only one solid ball left, and Kim is smirking at me.

But I run the table, then sink the eight ball with a long clean stroke. Between every shot I look over at the guy with the baby. The kid is happy now, on his third ride, and the guy just looks lost and bewildered.

Kim looks beautiful, and a big part of me wants to take her down on this pool table and wrestle until we're sweaty and exhausted.

Another part of me—the part I can't quite measure—wants to pick up that baby and find the Mobil girl, take both their hands, and help them.

The other part of me—the one that wins—makes me retreat inside, makes me shrivel. Makes me wonder if I'll ever do anything that matters.

Kim squeezes my arm and looks up at me (not many people can look up at me, but she's short enough), and says "Rack 'em up?"

I start to say "No, I'm tired," but I know that isn't true. So I say "Yeah, I'll play another game." It's healthier than playing games in my head.

Kim deposits a quarter to release the balls, then spends about two minutes racking them up, rearranging them about fifteen times.

I can see the guy sitting outside now with a cigarette, staring straight ahead, holding the baby on his knee. The kid is playing with the buttons on the guy's shirt, and the guy doesn't seem to realize that he's blowing smoke in the kid's hair.

Kim sinks one on the break, but doesn't leave herself much of a second shot. I sink five in a row before she shoots again, and I win on my next turn. I haven't said a word in ten minutes.

"You're good," Kim says.

I nod. "Sometimes." I force a smile on her, too, and start digging in my pocket for another quarter.

Things my father told me never to do:

* eat fish at the diner

* boo the other team

* marry the first woman you fall in
  love with

Things he never mentioned:

* how to change a spark plug

* why he goes to church

* if he ever misses his dad

.

CHAPTER 13

February

The moon is nearly full, and there's the slightest dusting of snow on the ground. The air is cold, but there's no wind, so the only sound is the frozen leaves crunching lightly under our feet.

My dad has a flashlight, but he hasn't turned it on. The last thing he said was back at the house when he asked if I wanted to come along. I nodded and put on a hooded sweatshirt and gloves. Mom's working tonight. I knew something was up, and I guess he knew that I knew.

We're headed for the houses by the pond, through the woods about a half-mile above our house. There are maybe two dozen little houses there; most of them aren't even winterized, and nobody lives in any of them except during the summer and the occasional weekend. My dad does maybe three jobs a year up there, ever since he was in high school. Once every year or two he takes me along, silently passing along a heritage that started with his own daddy.

The trees are tall back here, maples and white pine. We're high enough that I can see the lights of Sturbridge far below us. And I can see my breath.

My dad has his black-and-red-checked hunting jacket on, and a dark blue watch cap pulled low. He's carrying a small cloth sack with a drawstring. There's a dog barking way down below, and my lips are dry. We'll have a couple of beers together when we get back.

We come to a clearing above the pond and he stops. The pond is two football fields wide and three times as long. Tonight it's as black as coal, except where the moonlight shines like a mirror. It's frozen solid. Below us is a small beach, with two low docks jutting out into the water. On the far end of the pond is a Boy Scout camp, and lining either side are the cottages, owned by people from Brooklyn and Philadelphia and New Jersey. I've been inside a couple of them, on other nights like this.

"That red one," he says, and I wonder if he's been there before. I figure he must have hit all of these places at one time or another, but maybe he has his favorites. We start walking again, keeping our distance from the water and coming up behind the house.

There's a dirt road that circles the pond, and we walk it for about fifty yards. All the houses are dark. This one has a low rock wall that runs from the road to the water, lining one end of the property. I know the house. It's small and squarish, with a big picture window that looks out on the pond and a cinder-block chimney on the side. There's maybe a half cord of wood stacked against the house, which is a muddy red clapboard. My father tries the door for the hell of it, then walks to the window near the chimney.

It doesn't take much to get the window open, and he climbs in and motions me in after him. The house smells musty from being closed up since summer. He clicks on the flashlight and puts his hand over the light, running it slowly around the room.

We're in the kitchen, so he opens some cabinets and finds

a few cans of soup and a jar of spaghetti sauce. Nothing we'd want. He carefully shuts the cabinets and looks around. The inside of the refrigerator smells sour and moldy, so I shut the door as soon as I open it.

He takes a small clock radio from a bedroom, and also a hammer and a couple of fishing lures from the room next to the kitchen. We leave the clothing and the blankets and the books, which include *Cannery Row* and *Roger's Version*. Dad says he's already read them.

I reach for the flashlight, and my father lets it go. I shine it on two portraits in the tiny living room, hung together in a cardboard mat with two openings. The one on the left is Elvis in his youth, with slick black hair and a cocky smile; the other is the standard painting of Jesus you see everywhere. In a faint hand, someone had scrawled "You give me strength" in blue pencil on the cardboard.

We go back to the kitchen, and my father pulls open a drawer next to the sink. He finds eighty cents and two bottle openers. He holds up the openers, determines that they're exactly the same, and slips one into the sack. The other one goes back in the drawer.

"Been needing one of them," he says, holding the sack open and studying the contents. He bites down on his lip and looks up at the ceiling. "Last time I was here . . . I was twenty-four years old. Got a jackknife and two cans of motor oil." He rubs his chin, dark and scratchy with two days' growth. "Did better this time, I'd say."

We leave by the same window. He never does any damage, wouldn't even leave a drawer ajar, so it's likely that the owners will never know we were there. They'll look at each other one evening next June and wonder if they hadn't left a clock radio in that back bedroom, and old Sam will be confounded by what could have become of his hammer.

My father is good at this. So good that it's invisible to everyone but me. Like a ghost, spanning the decades, revisiting the past as he revisits old trespasses. It's his secret, and he shares it with me alone.

We move real quickly getting back to the trail through the woods, and my father lets out a triumphant little laugh when we finally reach safe ground.

"You ever worry about getting caught, Dad?"

"Not much. Got it down to a science." He puts a hand on my shoulder and we slow our pace. He shrugs, and laughs again, feeling giddy and renewed, I suppose.

Colleges I should have applied to:

   * Penn State

   * Kutztown

   * East Stroudsburg

   * Millersville

Colleges that I did:

CHAPTER 14

There's an envelope sticking out of my locker when I get to school. It's a valentine from Kim. I look at my watch. Yes, it's February 14, and it's 7:58. Rite Aid opens in two minutes, and homeroom begins in seven. I can make it.

I sprint out the door and down the hill, through the alley next to the bagel place and into the drugstore. I scan the cards and grab one with two rabbits on it—"Honey Bunny, Won't You Be Mine?"—and race to the register. The store has only been open for a minute and a half, but there's a lady at the checkout with two bottles of shampoo, a box of Motrin, four bars of Jergens facial soap, a tube of Crest, and an ironing board cover. Oh, and four coupons. Two of the coupons have expired, and a discussion begins. It's 8:04. I throw two dollars on the counter (the card cost a dollar twenty-five) and sprint out the door.

Mrs. Corcoran shoots me a look as I get in a minute late, but she doesn't say anything, since I'm usually prompt. Digit reaches over and takes the card and gives me a big shit-eating grin.

"I love you, too," he says. "I'll give you your present later."

"Give me that," I say. "That's for Al."

This is a huge day for me. Not because it's Valentine's Day, but because it's Wednesday: wrestle-off day. I'm 6–0 this season for real, but 0–8 in wrestle-offs.

I think I've finally got him figured out, though. Last week he beat me 7–3, but I was actually ahead 3–2 midway through the second period. And he hasn't pinned me in a month.

Al and Hatcher are ranked first in the state in their weight classes, and Digit is rated third at 130. And none of those guys is significantly better than I am.

I've been watching and waiting for a long time, getting my little half-ass matches but gearing up for something monumental.

The bell rings for first period and I go looking for Kim. Then I remember I haven't even opened her card.

I tear open the envelope and skip the verse. She wrote "Ben" on top and signed it "Love, Kim." I'd just signed "Ben" on hers. I keep a tight rein on my emotions.

I shut my eyes and wipe the sweat from my face, getting a grip on my nerves. I am so psyched I feel little explosions going off in my arteries, but I have to keep thinking clearly.

I'm ahead, 5–3, and I took Al down twice in the first period. He escaped the first time and took me down, but I managed to get free. Then I shot in and took him down again. I think I've got him rattled.

Coach waves me to the center circle; I start the period down. Very few people can survive from this position against Al, but I am ready. Coach blows the whistle and I force my way up, loosening his grip and escaping.

We circle around each other, and he keeps reaching for me, but I stay clear. Then I shoot in and grab his ankle, and he's down on his stomach and I have control. I am destroying him.

It's 8–3. Who's number one now? He escapes quickly and

takes me down, but I drag him out of bounds. I've still got the lead and the momentum.

I escape: 9–6. I take him down again—I have solved this man, I am ruining him. It is 11–6 and he's in trouble. I am rolling him to his back, rolling just too far, losing control, and he reverses me. It's 11–8, but the period's almost over; 11–8 and I know I can hold on till the whistle blows.

I don't succumb. I will start the third period up. I have taken him down four times in this match, and I doubt that anybody's ever done that to him. Not even when he was a freshman.

The third period begins. Make that five takedowns. He is down, I will win this thing today. I will ride him the whole period, and I will never look back. He is slippery; his muscles are smooth and sweaty and strong.

Somehow he gets loose. Somehow he gets to his feet and shoots in and puts me on my back. Somehow I'm ahead only 13–11 and he's got control.

Coach is hovering beside us, head against the mat, watching for a pin. But I will not be pinned. I will get out of this.

And I do, but not completely. I get off my back but can't quite escape, and he gets three near-fall points and the lead.

And that's as far as it goes. 14–13. The closest I've been in years.

I take off my headgear and shout "Shit!" so the whole school can hear it. I had it. I had him beat.

"Relax, Benny," Coach says. "What's your problem?"

I kick my headgear to the side of the mat. "I had him,

Coach," I say. "I had him beat."

Coach waves me over. Al's at the water fountain, and the 145-pounders are waiting to wrestle. Coach puts his hand on my shoulder.

"You feeling all right?" he asks.

"Just pissed."

"At who?"

"At myself. I had him beat, Coach. I had him beat."

Coach sort of smiles. "You wrestled good," he says. "But don't get bent out of shape, kid. It wasn't like you think."

I'm still seething. "What wasn't?"

"He needed to work on reversals. The state meet's coming up and he hasn't had enough challenges. Not many people ever take him down."

"Not like I did."

"Right. Not like you did. He needed four or five opportunities under real, live conditions. We talked it over before the match."

Suddenly, I get the picture. All the life goes out of me. I stand frozen on the mat, staring at the wall.

"He's the best in the state, Ben," Coach says softly. He puts his arm around me. "Get yourself a shower."

I head for the locker room. Al and Hatcher are wrestling on another mat, laughing and straining. Digit is refereeing.

I walk down the stairs like a zombie. I open my locker, put my clothes in my gym bag, and put my coat on over my wrestling stuff. I take the bag and lock the locker. I walk home real slow and unlock the house. Mom's already at work and my father hasn't gotten home yet. I go to my room and set the gym bag on the floor. I take off my wrestling shoes and turn off the light, and curl up on the bed with two fingers against my lips and my eyes open wide in the darkness. I don't know how long I lie there. Eventually, I fall asleep.

When I wake up, my father is standing over me with his hand on my forehead. "You okay?" he says.

I open my eyes. "Yeah. Getting a cold maybe."

"You eat anything?"

"No . . . What time is it?"

"About eight-thirty."

"Okay. I'll get something soon."

He goes back downstairs. My lips are dry and I am thirsty. My eyes sting a little, but I never stay sad for long. My sadness is already turning to anger. No way is it ending like this.

I watch the match against Midvale from the end of the bench, in street clothes. We win big, as expected, wrapping up a 16–0 dual-meet season. All that remains is the league meet and the state tournament.

I want to get home—I've barely spoken to anybody all day. Digit said "Good match yesterday" to me in homeroom and I told him to eat shit. I think he meant it though. He wouldn't bust my chops about that.

I head for the exit, and I hear Kim call my name pretty sharply. I stop and turn. I avoided her all day. She comes over.

"What's up?" she says.

"Not much," I answer.

"You going home?"

"I was."

"You said you'd call me last night."

I let out a sigh and start chewing on my lip. "I wasn't feeling very good."

"Still could have called."

We're in people's way, so I step against the wall. "I got my ass kicked again in the wrestle-off," I tell her. "I needed to be alone."

She stares straight ahead and starts to say something, then stops. Then she starts again. "You know, every time you have a shitty match you head for the door like a race horse. When things are going good, you're only too happy to see me. When you have a little problem, you act like I'm a pain in the butt."

"No, I don't."

"Like hell you don't. What am I, your cheerleader? I only get to come close when you want to feel like a hero?"

"I don't want to feel like a hero."

"No? What do you want, Ben? You don't seem to want me."

"Yes, I do."

"Not bad enough. . . . Maybe as an ornament."

I look away. Two little kids are wrestling out on the mat, and several groups of adults are standing around talking. The guy from the newspaper is interviewing Al and the coach.

"It was the worst wrestle-off of my life, Kim. The worst match I could imagine."

"What does that have to do with me?"

"Nothing. Everything. I don't know. I'm sorry."

She studies me a few seconds, probably wondering how she got hooked up with such a wimp. "Okay," she finally says.

I roll my tongue over my left molars and look at the floor. Then I look at Kim. She squints at me, and I touch her nose with one finger. My feet are cold and my head is hot. I feel like I'm going to throw up. One of her friends is standing by the door. She gives Kim a look like "Are you coming or not?"

"You going home?" Kim asks me again.

"Yeah," I say. "I really do feel shitty. Okay?"

"Okay." She smiles and touches my mouth with two fingers. "You jerk. I'll see you tomorrow."

"Happy Valentine's Day." And she is gone.

Questions I'm not ready to answer:

  * was that my last match?

  * is Kim going to give up on me?

  * could I handle being little Daniel's
    father?

Answers I'm not very fond of:

  * maybe.

  * maybe.

  * no way in hell.

I wasn't there, but I can envision it clearly. I know the procedure. I've been there before.

Winter in northeastern Pennsylvania is cold. The temperature falls to the teens in January and hardly ever gets out for at least eight weeks. Most nights it hits single digits.

The furnace generates a lot of heat every night, keeping the school warm for us students.

Picture Al with a six-pack, a not-so-unusual occurrence. He's driving around after practice with two other guys and two other six-packs. They get to talking about their English teacher, a prissy, balding guy in his thirties who still lives with his mother. They don't like him much.

The school's open—adult education classes going on downstairs—so they park the car and slip inside and make their way up to the classroom. This was Tuesday, about 8 P.M.

It was already down to 14 degrees.

If you piss on a radiator that's going full blast, then shut the classroom door tight, you'll have a pretty healthy odor in there by the following morning. It bakes on good. You can even wait fifteen minutes or so for the first layer to get sticky, then add another coat. Leave in a hurry, and don't make much noise on your way out.

If you're on the wasted side, you might get a little carried away. You might laugh uncontrollably, loud enough for somebody walking the halls to be alerted.

If that guy happens to be the vice principal, you're nailed.

Now Mr. Frazier is a decent man. He's a wrestling fan. He knows that the league meet starts on Friday, and he can take a joke as well as anybody.

But there's witnesses here. Can't strike a deal, even for the good of the program. All three guys have to go down together. Damn lucky it didn't happen next week. Next week is the districts. You miss the districts, your season is over. Missing the league meet is survivable.

It's a three-day suspension: Wednesday, Thursday, and Friday. If you don't wrestle in Friday's qualifying round, you obviously can't wrestle on Saturday.

Coach tries to make a deal, but there's no way out of this one. The official word is a violation of school rules. I'd love to see that rule in writing ("Students shall refrain from urinating on heating elements").

Al sits home, misses three days of school and practice. The entire town is alerted. If this was district week, there'd be a lynching.

I get to wrestle in the league meet.

1. STURBRIDGE (16–0). Last week's ranking: 1. Won 58th consecutive dual match. Al Phillips (135) and Anthony Hatcher (140) remained unbeaten.

2. CANONSBURG (14–1). Last week: 4. Upset then-No.2 Nazareth 30–25 on pin by unbeaten heavyweight Bill Lustig.

3. NORTHAMPTON (12–0–1). Last week: 5. Won two dual matches, including 34–21 over No. 9 Reading Eastside.

4. NAZARETH (16–1). Last week: 2. Lost first dual match in three seasons, 30–25 to Canonsburg.

5. MECHANICSBURG (17–0). Last week: 7. Had five individual winners in taking Allegheny Conference tournament title.

6. ALTOONA CENTRAL (12–2). Last week: Unranked. Routed then–No.3 Johnstown, 39–15. Once-beaten Lester DeBose pinned previously unbeaten Zach Elliott at 103.

7. EASTON (11–2–1). Last week: 8. Completed dual-meet season with two victories. Jordan Williams stayed unbeaten at 119.

8. PENN HILLS (13–1). Last week: 10. Claimed third straight Greater Pittsburgh Interscholastic League tournament.

9. READING EASTSIDE (9–3). Last week: 6. Defeated Tamaqua. Lost to Northampton.

10. JOHNSTOWN (15–1). Last week: 3. Lost to No. 6 Altoona Central.

I'm seeded second behind Arnie Kiefer of Laurelton, who's ranked fourth in the state and is the only guy in the league Al didn't pin this season. In fact, he gave Al the only close match he's had all year, 8–5, at their place back in January. I wrestled him last year and he pinned me in the first period.

If I meet him at all, it won't be until the final tomorrow. Tonight I've got a short guy with giant arms from Mount Ridge. Matches are going on on two mats, since they've got to get through four bouts in every weight class tonight.

Our stands are packed, but people have been noticeably quiet during the early matches. There are a lot of pissed-off adults who can't believe what happened to Al, who's like the second coming of. . . Jerry Franken, at least. Coach took some heat, but I think most people are convinced that he's not at fault. They realize he stood with unflinching valor in Al's defense but lost. I'm catching some cold looks as I warm up, as if I'm somehow to blame for not being Al.

Folks, I'm 6–0. I'm in the greatest shape of my life and I'm hungry. Forget Al for two days. He'll survive.

I get out on the mat and we shake hands. This guy's arms, I may have mentioned, are out of proportion, long and thick and heavy. So his thighs are skinny, and he's got no butt. His hair is short and light.

The ref blows the whistle and I shoot really low, under those arms, and grab him about the knees. I put him down.

I twist him around and drive him toward the mat, and he is helpless and outclassed and in trouble.

Twenty-three seconds and he's fried. I barely worked up a sweat. I unsnap my headgear, shake his hand again without looking at him, and retreat into the locker room.

I've got the guy from North in the semifinals tomorrow afternoon. I want no contact with anybody until then.

We advanced all thirteen weights into the semis; no other team moved more than eight. The team title looks like a lock. The crowd seems more relaxed today, looser and louder. The Al thing may be forgotten, for now.

Tommy Austin made the final at 103, and our guys also won semis at 112 and 125. Digit's finishing up his semi right now. He's got a big lead, but it doesn't look like he'll pin the guy.

Coach hasn't said anything to me except to do the best I can. I just nodded. I stayed awake most of the night, listening to the radio, and finally fell asleep about three. But I'm not tired. Every muscle feels wide awake, energized. I'm up next.

Al is sitting on the bottom row of the stands, wearing his letterman's jacket, which he almost never wears. He's got his chin in his hand, watching intently but not saying much. He's sitting with some football players, but I saw him come in alone. He brightens just a little when I catch his eye. He's got his hair combed.

The guy from North is taller than I am, which is not in his favor. I'm compact—I've got a low center of gravity. Tall, thinner guys never do well against me. This guy is dead meat. He's got straight dark hair and eyes that are too close together. His hands are big and sweaty; he can't seem to get a grip on me. When I throw him to the mat, his air rushes out and his cheeks get red and blotchy. The ones who shut their eyes as you twist them never seem to recover. The end comes fifty-five seconds into the match.

Coach puts his arm around me as I walk off the mat. "Good one," he says. "You can win it all, you know."

I know. I grab my squirt bottle and take off the headgear. Hatcher pats my shoulder. Digit shakes my hand and won't let go. "Al was supposed to give you three takedowns, then pin you, you know," he says. "Think about it, Ben. He couldn't do it."

Kim intercepts me on the way to the locker room.

"Hey, stud," she says.

I probably turn red. I smile. "Hey," I say.

"You're not wasting any time, are you?"

"No." I reach to scratch myself, but stop. "Tonight's a different story. These first two guys were lame."

"See you after?"

"I'll try." I give her a weak smile and turn away. The only thing in my head for the next four hours should be Arnie Kiefer of Laurelton.

We have nine wrestlers in the finals. The pep band is in its finest form, unrolling all of its hits and debuting the theme from *Rocky*. Every seat is full, and lots of people are standing against the walls. I'm sitting next to Digit and we can barely hear each other talk. I'm not saying a whole lot anyway.

Tommy Austin wins at 103—the first freshman league

champion in sixteen years. We get seconds at 112 and 125, and Digit pins his guy in the third period. He's 24–1.

It gets a little quiet now. People are remembering that 135 ought to be the biggest lock of the tournament. Unbeaten Al on his home mat for the last time in his career.

Kiefer is one of these guys who looks bored and vicious at the same time. Like a junior Marine officer—cold, clear eyes, square jaw, tight mouth he never seems to open. He seems bigger, wider than a 135-pounder. The guy is 21–1 this season. Al just outsmarted him in January.

Three images whip through my mind in the seconds before the start: Reverend Fletcher, pale and paunchy, telling me about the evils of wrestling ("Foolish," he called it one Sunday last September. "Mean-spirited and aggressive"); this crowd, just minutes ago, rising to its feet and exulting in little Tommy Austin, the emerging hero, the man who'll carry this town through the next three cold winters; and me, staring at the ceiling last night in the darkness, imagining what the coming few minutes would offer.

I'm out there. The match starts. I hear Digit's voice above the others.

This man is strong. Stronger than Al, I'm certain, but not as quick, not as slippery. He's harder to move, but easier to control when you do. He's beatable.

He pinned me a year ago, when I was still in awe about wrestling varsity, scared of this guy's limited reputation, unable to let myself go. Tonight I let go. Tonight I let the crowd's rising crescendo carry me. I take him down, and my energy level seems to triple as the crowd roars its approval. I feel excitement in my muscles, the power of a thousand screaming voices. I feel strength I've never had before, and I feel this guy wilting beneath me.

Thirty-seven seconds and he is pinned. *Wham.* I raise both fists above my head. I shut my eyes and feel holy.

Coach rushes out to meet me, and Digit and Hatcher embrace me. I look to the stands, zero in on Al. "You're next, sucker," I say, thrusting a finger in his direction. He looks stunned and then angry. He scowls and makes a slapping motion with his hand.

Later they give me the Most Outstanding Wrestler trophy—three first-period pins. First minute, even. We won seven finals, including five straight from 130 to 152.

The locker room is a madhouse. Hatcher is on top of the lockers, naked, throwing balls of wet toilet paper at people. The music is on full volume and Digit is dancing outside the shower. Coach comes up to me and says, "That was a great way to cap your career, Benny. Really nice."

"One more," I say. "At least."

"Come on," he says with a smile. "Don't spoil it. You know better."

I shake my head, but I don't push the issue. He can't stop me from wrestling off with Al on Wednesday and he knows it. I'll deal with that later. Right now I'm too up.

Al comes in eventually and looks at my trophy. "What was that shit?" he says, meaning my action after the match.

This won't bring me down either. "Nothing," I say, but I meet his eyes for once. "Nothing personal."

"I'll kick your ass," he says, leaning against my locker.

"Might," I say. "Might not."

"I'll destroy you in front of everybody, pal," he says. "Don't even bother."

"Kiefer thought so, too."

"Kiefer sucks. He's nothing. You won't last thirty seconds with me, Ben."

I don't like this much. Me and Al have been friends for six years. I'm as good as I am because I've been wrestling him every day. But that cuts the other way, too.

He starts to walk away, looking straight ahead and jabbing his hands in his pockets. "I'll kick your ass," he says.

It comes to me now: Al is scared. He may be the best high school wrestler in this state—everybody who knows seems to think so.

I think so, too. But there's one guy left who can take him. One guy who really believes he can do it.

And that guy used to be Al's best friend.

I get dressed in a hurry and go looking for Kim. She's waiting in the hallway. This time I'm glad to see her.

Things that won't happen in the
wrestle-off:

  * he won't embarrass me

  * I won't get pinned

  * we won't both be happy when it's
    over

Things that could:

  * I could get slaughtered

  * I could get my arm busted

  * I could be the best in the state

FOR THE ANGEL OF THE LORD DESCENDED FROM HEAVEN

AND ROLLED BACK THE STONE FROM THE DOOR

AND SAT UPON IT.

HIS COUNTENANCE WAS LIKE LIGHTNING

AND HIS RAIMENT WHITE AS SNOW.

That's what it says on the stone above Giles Greene (Nov 9 1823–Aug 14 1892). I'm reading it while Kim tightens her shoe. She's got on black running tights and a light-blue sweatshirt with the hood down. And big gray mittens. It's the first day above freezing in at least a month. There's been hardly any snow this winter, so the ground is firm and bare.

She stands up and starts running again. Most of my friends won't run in the cemetery because of some general dread of death. I think it's the most peaceful place in town, a great place to work out or just walk through and think. It's in the wooded hills on the far side of the river, with blue spruce and hemlocks and some giant white pines.

We run on dirt paths between the graves, surrounded by names of families that died out a century ago—Penwarden, Farnham, Tibbetts—and names of families I see every day—Tryon, Kimble, McFarland.

Last night me and Kim and Digit just hung out on Main Street after the match, talking about little things, like TV shows or where we might get jobs this summer. And the whole time my mind was trying to figure out how to do it, how to beat Al in the wrestle-off. And I went to sleep last night knowing I would do it, and I woke up this morning knowing that I wouldn't.

We curve around past an old family plot with a low metal fence—just foot-high posts with a railing—and run uphill toward the Civil War area. There's a ring of gravestones there, maybe two dozen. Sometimes in the summer we'd take Pabst Blue Ribbon from Al's refrigerator and sit among those stones at night, looking up at the stars. Those were always good times; we'd never get rowdy in the cemetery. We'd just sit there and talk about our fathers, why we love them and why we hate them. Why we'd do anything in our power to avoid being like them, and somehow knowing that we already are.

Kim stops to read one of the stones. "'John Baker, Co. C,'" she says. "Company C, I guess . . . "

She bends over to look at another, and I'm taken by the view of her slender thighs under spandex. "This one was a corporal," she says. "'Jas. Northcott.'"

There's lichen on all these stones; some are cracked and chipped. We head down the hill, not saying much, just taking it in, the peace.

She runs faster down the gentle slope, opening her stride and moving away from me. I can never run that gracefully, that effortlessly. Even sprinting now she looks so smooth, like a doe pulling away from me, or a dancer, her dark hair bouncing on her shoulders.

She circles back to me after a minute, panting but smiling. "Sorry," she says. "I just felt so good. I had to take off."

"No problem," I say, falling back in step with her. "You look strong."

"Yeah. Thanks," she says. "I love to run fast. Just to let everything go. I can't wait to start racing this spring."

We keep running, sticking to the older section, making half-mile loops on the paths. The newer section is flatter and less wooded, less interesting. I found my grandfather's stone in there last summer: my father's father. He died when I was little and nobody ever took me to the grave. It says he fell asleep in the arms of Jesus, but that isn't the way I heard it.

My mother says she never saw the guy without a drink in his hand. I guess that's an exaggeration, but I see her point.

Kim drives a little harder up a hill, but jogs in place at the top to wait for me. "I love it in here," she says quietly, almost at a whisper. "I feel so connected with the past. It makes me feel so alive."

At the bottom of the slope she stops to look at another stone, a big one. "This guy was a doctor," she says. "'Samuel E. and Lucretia B. Dunning. Died 1877, 1881.'" She drops to her knees and looks at a smaller stone behind it, squinting to read the faded words. "'Our Charlie. June 21 1862–January 3 1863.' . . . Oh. . . . That's so sad."

She stands and takes a step toward me, still staring at the little stone. She slowly brushes her hair back from her forehead. I resist an urge to put my arm around her, to hold her. I look up at the sun, then back at the stone, then over at Kim, who walks toward another marker. And I'm struck by the simplest of thoughts: how real Kim is. Real to me, I mean. Not like the images I've had in my head of other women; of Jody, the Mobil girl, of girls I'd watch in school or on the street, or even of Kim up to this point. Suddenly, the fantasies are over. For the first time in my life I don't need them just now. Because she's real and she's here and I can deal with it.

The sun goes behind a cloud, and I walk over to Kim, who's studying a marker from 1844. Another simple thought; this one I say out loud: "This seems like a good place to be a hundred years from now, don't you think? Nothing really left but some lines etched in stone."

Kim looks up at me, just gazing at my face. "Makes you think," she says softly, "about what has to come first." I put my hand on top of her head and tap her gently with my fingers. She leans forward slightly and rests her forehead on my chest. And I don't say what I'm feeling, because it seems premature, but I let out my breath and rest my chin on her head and let my arms drop down around her shoulders.

We stand there like that for a couple of minutes, silent. The workout is over. Kim raises her head. We walk back toward town, toward the future.

CHAPTER 18

Wednesday. I wrestle Al this afternoon. Winner goes to the districts, the other guy goes home. I meet Kim at lunch and we walk down to the Main Street Deli. There are some booths there, so we get sandwiches and sit down. I stare at my chicken salad on a hard roll with lettuce and tomato, and she says I better eat or I'll be weak later.

I take a deep breath and one bite.

"That's how I felt before the states in cross-country," she says. "I couldn't eat; I didn't sleep the night before." She makes me look up at her. "I came in a hundred and forty-sixth."

I pick up a chunk of the chicken from my plate and eat it. There's a pretty big crowd at the counter now, so it's a good thing we got here early. Mostly kids from school, a couple of lawyers, some secretaries.

"You wanna know why I punched that minister?"

She raises her eyebrows a little, nods. So I tell her.

Me and my father were coaching a team in this Sunday afternoon, little-kid soccer program. Our church put it on, but anybody could play. We had a team in the first- and second-grade league. Reverend Fletcher was one of the other coaches. Four teams, you play everybody else twice. The idea was to have fun and learn something. No standings or statistics. Purely instructional. Everybody plays an equal amount and everybody rotates positions.

So we're 1–2–1 after four weeks, and we're going against Fletcher's team, which is 4–0 and has clobbered everybody. He took all the best players for his team when he made up the rosters. Plus he knows the game—played in high school and all. No big deal, right? It's just for fun.

Anyway, after three quarters we're actually ahead, 3–2. We've got eight on each team, but it's a small field and you only play five at a time. Our best kids have already played two quarters, and so have his. So we send our subs back in.

He's got his guys huddled up on the sidelines. They're only about ten yards away from us, and we hear him telling these kids that if they don't win, then nobody goes to The Fun Zone afterward. Then he sends his best players back onto the field. They score four more goals and we never even get the ball past midfield.

Now, it isn't that we lost. The kids aren't even upset about it, they just love to play. All the kids shake hands, and he comes over to us to do the same. He takes my hand, and I say something like "That wasn't exactly fair to our guys." He keeps hold of my hand and frowns, then grips it a little tighter. I'm not smiling when I ask, "Does it really mean that much to you?"

"Don't be a poor loser, Ben," he says, and I tell him to screw himself. He shoves me away from him, and my father steps forward and sticks an arm between us. The Reverend is standing there kind of defiantly, holding his ground, and a couple of parents who'd been watching are inching their way over.

I hold my ground, too, and I tell him he's one hell of an example for these kids. "Darn right I am," he says. And then he calls me a pansy.

Now, I don't think anybody's actually used that as an insult in the past three or four decades, but I catch his intention. So I step forward again, right in his face (he's about five inches taller than me, but you know what I mean).

"Step back, son," he says.

I move about two inches closer. He shoves me with both hands, and I go at him swinging. It's over in a second, but I hit him once in the gut and a real solid right to the mouth that draws blood. I don't think he hit me at all.

My father and some other guys drag me away, but I shake loose and just walk toward the car. My father catches up and doesn't say anything right away, just walks alongside me, looking back once or twice. When we get in the car, he sighs and grips the wheel and nods at me nonstop for about thirty seconds. He punches me gently on the arm—I'm still seething—and says, "Well, let's get home." He starts the car and we're out of there, and he's got a hint of a smile he's trying to hide.

He's never mentioned it again.

Kim's got her arms folded kind of tight and she's looking at me like she doesn't quite get it. But she's got that same hint of a smile that my father had, and I don't think I've ruined her image of me.

"So," she says. "Can you call back enough of that anger to help you this afternoon against Al?"

"I'm not sure I have any of that anger left," I say. "But I don't have to look too far to find more. I can get set off when I need to."

"Why do you need to?" She's unfolded her arms.

"I'm not sure that I do. But I still have plenty. Plenty of anger. Frustration."

I reach my hand across the table and put it on top of hers. I squeeze her hand gently and look in her eyes, and she smiles kind of stoically.

"Why don't you put all that anger in one little package and take it onto the mat with you today?" she says. "And use it all up, every ounce of it. Then, win or lose, walk away and move on."

I withdraw my hand but not my eyes, and I smile and let out my breath. Then I start eating what's left of my sandwich, and she puts her foot on top of mine under the table. I put down the sandwich, wipe my mouth on my sleeve, and go around to her side of the booth, where I sit right against her, put my arm around her—probably getting chicken salad that I just wiped off my mouth on her shirt—and kiss her really nice on the lips.

Now how am I gonna get angry again by this afternoon?

What happens before a match (in this order):

* diarrhea and mood swings

* a kind of prayer where you curse at God and beat yourself up, then tell God you're sorry and he says it's okay

* a concentrated sense of focus

What doesn't:

* you don't joke around with anybody

* you don't resign yourself to losing

* you never say it doesn't matter what happens

They've moved the wrestle-offs to the main gym, and they've had to let the bleachers down on both sides of the court because of the crowd. In my four years here I've never seen more than fifteen spectators at the wrestle-offs. Today there must be seven hundred.

Al's already out there warming up, but we won't be wrestling for about twenty minutes. I'm sitting in front of my locker with my sweatshirt hood pulled up, just staring at my hands and exhaling pretty hard. I've got a scar on the back of my left hand, barely visible unless you know where to look, from when I ripped it open playing kickball on the playground in third grade. Fell face-first heading for second, but the only injury I remember is my hand. You could see bone at the knuckles.

I lie flat on the bench, clenching my fists.

The ceiling in this locker room is high, and we get big clouds of steam bouncing around up there after practice when all the showers are going. Somebody, years ago, must have climbed on top of the lockers, took a pen, and wrote STURBRIDGE SUCKS on the ceiling in the corner. Maybe it was my father.

There are people who've asked me to concede this match, to not even wrestle. Why stand in Al's way, they want to know. Why risk getting him hurt?

There are a few people who want me to win, though. Some guys on the team, maybe even Digit; I haven't asked. I've been waiting a long time to walk out there in a match that means everything—my whole career. Al's, too. I earned it and I want it.

There are people out there watching who don't know who they'll be pulling for. They won't know until we're out there, when the first move gets made, and they'll wince or revel without even knowing it and then they'll find out who they're for.

If I was watching, that's how I'd be. But I won't be watching. So I'm pulling for me.

Tommy Austin beat Anthony Terranova pretty good in the first match, and Larry Drummond pinned his guy at 119. There are no challenges at 125 or 130, so me and Al are up.

Al is staring at me from across the mat, and Coach is waving us out there. Al is pissed. He's 22–0 and nothing should be standing between him and the states.

But somebody is. And I'm pissed, too.

I got down 2–0 almost before I had time to react. Al shot in and got me up in the air, flipping me onto my back so I was in immediate trouble. I twisted and tried to get out of bounds because he already had the leverage he needed, but he yanked me back toward the center of the mat and started forcing me down. He wanted to get this over with, and he was being more aggressive than even he'd ever been.

He got near-fall points, but I managed to squirm out of it and get back to my knees. Five–nothing, and he was still riding me. It took most of the period for me to work my way free, but I finally got to my feet and escaped just in time. Five–one, I was behind.

Al didn't even leave the mat between periods. He just squatted with his hands on his knees and stared at the big blue S in the center circle, breathing hard. I walked off and grabbed a squirt bottle from Digit. Coach didn't look at me.

I started the second period down, but escaped pretty quickly. Al does that. He'll give up an escape point to get two in return with a takedown. Usually when he lets a guy go, he gets an evil smirk, kind of half-circles the guy, then goes in for the kill. But he came right back at me and threw me to the mat without any nonsense, and suddenly I was down 7–2 with his nails digging into my skin.

For the next minute and a half he rode me, trying to get me cradled, to bring my shoulders to the mat. But he couldn't do it this time. Coach even started to warn us for stalling, since we were barely moving, but my effort was maximum, and Al's was, too. We just seemed to be on neutral ground all of a sudden, deadlocked. The second period ended and I was down by only five points.

Al was still mad, but it wasn't just at me anymore. He was pissed at himself, I know, because this was going far too long and there didn't seem to be much he could do about it. It'd been a long time since he got tested like this. And now my confidence was escalating, too. I was seething. Seething in a good way, a way I knew what to do with.

I scanned the bleachers, looking for Kim and half expecting one of those movie-type breakthroughs where I'd catch her eye and feel a lightning bolt of energy and desire that would carry me to victory.

Instead, I saw my father, and the impact was different but the same. He was standing about three-quarters of the way up, arms folded, looking kind of dazed. I didn't try to catch his eye. I tried to share his dignity.

I started the third period up, and Al was tensed below me, ready to explode to his feet the instant Coach blew the whistle. Maybe it's a cliché, but my life had come down to a two-minute summary: the third period of this match. There was life on the other side: Kim, an escape from this town, my pride. But there was too much value in what had gone before to let it fade away without a defining moment. That moment had arrived.

Al is pale, like sweaty marble coiled beneath me. The whistle blows, and instead of forcing up, he drops to the mat on his belly. My grip slips away. He rolls, and I grab the back of his thigh, jabbing my other arm over his shoulder. He gets to his knees. Coach gives him an escape point, but I swing up behind him and regain control. I've got him in a half nelson and I'm pushing with everything I have. Now he's down.

I'm behind 8–4, but there's a chance here. Al is on the mat, facedown, and every muscle in his back is flexed and extended. His right shoulder is coming up, it has no choice, because at this crucial moment I'm stronger than he is. I have to lift him and turn him, and I give back an inch for every two that I gain. But I'm gaining, and he's groaning, and suddenly he's perpendicular—his left shoulder is digging into the mat, his right is at a 90-degree angle toward the ceiling.

That angle is growing shorter as I force him toward the mat. One hand is gripping my chest, but he has no leverage at all, no power. Time is getting short. Coach is kneeling beside us, palm flat, watching for that moment when both of Al's shoulders are planted firmly against the mat.

The crowd sounds frantic, but maybe they're enjoying this. I am up on my toes, pushing hard, using my knees and my gut and my thighs and my shoulders. I taste his sweat; he is pulling at my jersey and his headgear is slipping to one side. I don't know what's holding him up. It's my desperation versus his.

"Thirty seconds," somebody yells; Digit it was. Is he telling Al to hold on or urging me to find something more, to finish this thing? I give one mighty surge, everything I've got left. He moves closer to the mat, but not close enough.

I surge again and get nowhere, but I'm three inches from ending this thing, from pinning Al and walking away and moving on to where he'll never go. By sheer gravity I should win this now, all other things being equal.

But he's defying gravity. He's defying me, too. "Ten seconds," I hear, but ten minutes wouldn't be enough. I give one final surge. Coach blows his whistle. "Three," he says. It's over. Al lets go, lies flat on his back. I shut my eyes and get to my knees.

Eight–seven. Digit pulls me up. The bleachers are nearly full, and everyone is standing. Al shakes my hand, I clasp his arm and we walk off the mat. Coach calls the next wrestlers onto the floor.

It's over.

CHAPTER 22

My father's shaking my hand, too choked up to say anything, then handing me a twenty-dollar bill and telling me to take Kim out for dinner; I can take his car and he'll walk home. "No, really," he says. "Go. Get a shower and take this pretty girl out on me. You were great."

She's got tears in her eyes and the next match hasn't started yet; everybody's standing, cheering for Al and some for me, too. Coach is shaking his head and he's got a big grin, talking to the guy from the newspaper. Al and his father are hugging each other over by the water fountain. Digit's standing next to me, patting my back.

The pep band starts in with "You Can Call Me Al," brassy and off-key just a little. Al raises his fist in the air; there's a crowd around him now. My father musses my hair and mumbles "See ya at home," then turns to leave. Digit says "Gotta see Al," and he goes, so I hug Kim and kiss her on the forehead. Coach blows his whistle and the 145-pounders attack each other. The band shuts up.

Kim waits in the stands and I go to the locker room. Nobody's in there. I shower a long time, letting the heat soak into my chest and through my head and down to my feet. My season's over, but I've got shampoo left. I'll have to go out for track.

I'm thinking Chinese food would be good; fried rice and snow peas, maybe with shrimp. My father doesn't have any decent tapes in his car. I'll borrow one from somebody. I love

Kim. Digit has some good tapes in his locker. Al will win the states, no question.

The 189ers are wrestling by the time I get up there, and there's almost nobody left in the stands. I sit next to Digit, who's sitting next to Kim, and she and I hold hands behind his back until the last wrestle-off is over. We give him a ride home and then head to the Chinese Kitchen in Weston.

Digit's tape sounds good, even with the cheap speakers in this vehicle. Kim has her hair in a ponytail. She is looking happy. This is a day I will never forget.

I get home late. My father is asleep on the couch, and the TV is on, but it's turned so soft you can barely hear it. Mom's still at work.

I climb the stairs quietly—I'll let her be the one to wake him—and shut my door before turning on the light. It's just cold enough outside, so I take off my jacket and put on two sweatshirts, as much for comfort as for warmth.

I can taste Kim's mouth and her skin. I smell her soft hair and feel her sweet, moist breath on my neck. And I feel Al's muscles, hard as steel and flexible as good strong rope, and I feel his breath on my skin, too, cursing, straining, finally wanting it as much as I did.

I sit on my bed to change from my running shoes to hiking boots, and then I see it there on the wall. The Elvis and Jesus thing from that house by the lake, with "You give me strength" scrawled on the cardboard matting.

I stand and take a step toward it and stop, not sure whether to laugh or to shudder or feel honored.

I shut the light and stand in the hallway in silence, with my hands in the big pouch pocket of the sweatshirt. Then I walk down the stairs to my father. I touch him lightly on the shoulder and he rolls, opening his eyes and looking surprised. "Thanks, Dad," I say.

"Oh . . . yeah," he says, sitting up and rubbing one eye with his hand. "Just, you know . . . I don't know."

"Yeah," I say. "I know." We stare at the TV for a few seconds, then I turn to the door. "I'm just going for a walk," I finally say. I haven't been alone yet, to absorb this day, to make it permanent.

The woods are quiet, but my vision is good. The moon is out and shining. This was a day. This can be the day Al begins reliving his father's life, or the day he breaks free. I think of Hatcher—too dumb to be a doctor like his dad, but just dumb enough to relive everything else about him. Only Digit is sure to break the pattern. Me, I don't know.

I can see the lights of the town far below me, and a dog is barking in the distance. My father is asleep again by now, snoring on the couch with the TV on softly. He'll be punching in at the plant in eight hours.

I look at the moon, and it's right where it should be, a quarter million miles away. I stop walking and shut my eyes in the cool, clear breeze, lifting my arms above my head and inhaling. The air smells piney, with just a hint of cows and of midnight.

Life is good. I have Kim.

I am tired and warm and alive.

Don't miss

PLAYING WITHOUT THE BALL
by Rich Wallace

Here's what they can list under my mug in the yearbook:

> Early-morning basketball, late-night hamburger chef, weekend basketball, honorary Methodist, weeknight basketball, background vocalist, playground basketball, voluntary orphan.

If I make the team, they can add varsity basketball, but I know the odds are against me. I'm a decent player, but I don't quite fit the system. I don't quite fit anywhere, so I live alone above a bar and work part-time in the kitchen to pay the rent. My father's gone to California to straighten himself out, so I'm left to bounce my life off Spit, a punk-rock genius who has bigger problems—but bigger potential—than I have.

I could join my father in L.A. if I wanted to, but I'm not ready to leave yet. I've got chances here—with girls, with basketball. And if those don't work out, I just might step from the shadows, join Spit on stage, and see if I can cut it as a singer.

You never know.

An ALA Best Book for Young Adults
An ALA Quick Pick for Young Adults

Half a block from the Turkey Hill convenience store, there's a town bench. And lately, if I'm not in school or at soccer practice, chances are I'm sitting there, thinking, for a lot of reasons.

For one thing, my best friend, Joey—the jerk—has a girlfriend now, the girl he knew I was after. And then there's soccer. Me and Joey are the backbone of the first strong soccer team our school's ever had, and we've got a chance to win the league this season. But that'll take teamwork, and that's the one thing we're missing.

Joey hogs the ball *and* gets the girls. But he's always been there for me—until now. Or maybe I'm just tired of being there for him. I suppose we ought to grow up. Maybe we'd win more soccer games.

"An excellent choice for all those boys who want only sports books, this is also a good read for any teen, male or female."   *—Booklist*

"Wallace's ear for locker-room banter . . . shines through in his vibrant characterizations."   *—Publishers Weekly*

"A deftly written book, and a solid addition to any YA collection."
—School Library Journal